WARRIOR GOD

"The battle is over," Semele wailed. "We have lost two men."

Looking at the chief, Casca realized that he had indeed already surrendered. He drew his .38, clapped it to the head of the nearest man and blew out his brains.

There was one great communal shriek, then silence. Casca pointed his little revolver at the man with the wounded arm and shot him through the heart, then turned the gun on Semele.

"This weapon needs no reloading," he lied. "One more word of surrender and I will kill you."

The Casca series
by Barry Sadler

THE WARRIOR

BARRY SADLER   **#17**

JOVE BOOKS, NEW YORK

CASCA #17: THE WARRIOR

A Jove Book / published by arrangement with
the author

PRINTING HISTORY
Charter edition / February 1987
Jove edition / September 1987

ISBN: 0-515-09603-2

Jove Books are published by The Berkley Publishing Group,
200 Madison Avenue, New York, New York 10016.
The name "JOVE" and the "J" logo
are trademarks belonging to Jove Publications, Inc.

PRINTED IN THE UNITED STATES OF AMERICA

10   9   8   7   6   5   4   3   2   1

CHAPTER ONE

Mountains of water swept the small schooner along on its crests. The masts were bare of sails; only one small triangular sail bellied from the forestay to provide some steerage way. In the stern Andrew Larsen stood wrestling with the helm, its length locked under his right armpit, the handle grasped in both his massive hands.

Around him his crew clung to the companionway and the two cabin skylights. All ten crew were on deck, as they preferred to be in such a storm, matching their skills and experience with the elements rather than suffering the effects below decks.

Chou Lui, the Chinese cook, stood facing Larsen, his short, fat legs spread wide, his arms folded, his back against the skylight. Now and then his impassive face would tilt upward to port or to starboard, indicating a giant following wave threatening to break over the stern.

Some of these seas did come thundering over the taffrail, burying the captain to his waist and forcing Chou Lui and the others to hang on for dear life as the deck disappeared under two feet of water.

Larsen managed to maneuver the *Rangaroa* away from the worst of these effects thanks to Chou's silent warnings, which left him free to concentrate on steering the bow on a

1

path through the waves that would best keep the ship upright.

To get the bow crosswise to a wave could put the *Rangaroa* on her beam ends, and should a second wave catch her while she was lying thus, the voyage would very quickly be over.

The attention of the other nine men was on the rigging, on the deck cargo and its lashings, and on the whaler secured atop the forward cabin. Should the single sail tear in the huge winds, the crew would leap to secure the flying tatters and bend another sail to the halyard. And should anything else, no matter what, come loose, they would be after it as one.

A sailing ship was like a living creature, a functioning organism where every rope and spar and pin contributed to its integrity and stability. If a shroud or stay should part, it could result in the loss of a mast. A lashing coming loose could set the deck cargo free to smash its way around the decks, breaking rails and tearing ropes free from their vital functions. And should the whaler break loose, it could well be stove in and rendered useless before it could be resecured.

Like Larsen, most of the crew were Europeans, professional seamen who preferred the dangers of the South Pacific to the safer, smaller waters of the Atlantic and the Mediterranean, where their homes had been. The seas here were bigger, storms more sudden and much more violent, but the rewards were sweeter too. The islands of the South Pacific were the last places on earth to be exploited, and their wealth was carried to the market places of Europe and the New World by ships such as the *Rangaroa*. The skies were sunny all year round—hot days, warm nights—and there were beautiful, golden-bodied women to share them with.

Below decks there was one man, the only passenger. But he had no interest in the niceties of steering a ship through a storm, nor in securing cargo or lifeboats.

Case Rafferty Lonnergan, who had started life almost two thousand years earlier as Casca Rufio Longinus, no longer had any interest even in the curse laid upon him by the Nazarene whose life he had plucked out on the cross with his Roman spear.

Casca was convinced that the curse must now be about to end, that at any moment the man he had killed on Golgotha, if he were a man, would appear. Perhaps he was even one of the *Rangaroa*'s crew. Casca knew that Jesus had been a fisherman of sorts when he wasn't preaching. Strange occupation for a carpenter's boy.

He recalled the words of the dying Christ: "Soldier, you are content with what you are, then that you shall remain until we meet again."

For the many hundreds of years since that afternoon in Palestine, Casca had fought and suffered and never been allowed to die. His many-scarred hide bore the marks of dozens of wounds that should have killed him—had killed him, but only for relatively short times, for days, or weeks or months that had passed like moments in a dream. But this was different. Now he knew he was really dying.

He rolled to the edge of the bunk and lolled his head over the side, trying to vomit, but only a few drops of watery dribble came from his mouth. He groaned and lay back.

Yes, he thought, it makes sense. The one who had said he was the son of God had cursed him to remain a soldier until he came again. He was doomed to walk the earth, fighting other men's battles, participating in other people's wars—an eternal mercenary, an eternal soldier—until Jesus came again, allowing him to pass on into everlasting eternity, and finally, peace. And now that his last agony was really here, of course he was not dying as a soldier. He had been in no battle, suffered no wounds. The sea itself was killing him. God's mightiest ocean was tossing the life out of his suffering body, rolling the ship from side to side so that his eyes rolled in his head as if, when the ship lay on her side, they might meet in the one socket.

Then, slowly, the ship would straighten up, the weight of its lead keel swinging it erect, the masts moving faster and faster until they were vertical and Casca lay on his back, staring at the planks of the overhead. But the ship rolled on, the insides of Casca's body rolling with her, until the tug of the small storm sail pulled her back. Then she would come erect once more before lying down in the sea again.

At the same time, she pitched fore and aft as the huge seas lifted her stern, rolled under her, then lifted her bow and dropped it as they rolled on their way. And Casca's insides would be lifted, too, then dropped as though forever, then jerked up again by the next wave. Or worst of all, his innards would be smashed down farther inside his body as an enormous following sea broke under the stern, lifting the whole of the ship itself from the sea. Sometimes one of these following seas would break on the deck, burying the ship, crushing it down, and Casca would feel his insides floating free inside his body.

If he could have seen topside at these moments, he would have felt better. A quick and merciful drowning was certain. The whole of the ship—the crew, the deckhouses, the cargo, the whaler, everything except the two masts and the tiny foresail—disappeared under the sea, and for what seemed like an eternity the sea held her there beneath the hundreds of tons of water.

But at last the wave would roll on its way and another would lift the buoyant *Rangaroa* up and up and up, until she was perched on its peak, racing along with the wave.

At these times Casca felt his entrails trying to leave his body by way of his rectum. And a second later, as the ship plunged down the steep face of the sea, it seemed his guts must exit his body by way of his mouth.

He didn't care. The irrelevant details of his imminent death didn't concern him. This wave must surely be the last. Alive yet? Then this one. And still alive? Well, this one then. But alive yet now? How many times could one suffer this death and still live?

The horrible thought came to him that the vengeance of the fisherman guru was now to become even worse than it had already been. He had died dozens of times in two thousand years, and now, was he to die dozens of times in a day? For how long?

He heard a stair creak and turned his head toward the companionway, opening his eyes a slit.

Now, he thought to himself, he comes to gloat. What will the son of God look like this time?

A pair of sea boots were followed by an oiled silk smock, but the face was that of Sandy, the wiry young ordinary seaman in the port watch.

"Are you feeling any better, matey?" the Scot asked cheerfully as he moved through to the galley. Returning in a moment with an armful of beef jerky and ship's biscuits, he said, "Man, we're all starvin' up there, and it looks like it'll last for hours more, or days." He threw a handful of biscuits onto the bunk. "Here, matey, try and chew on these, you'll feel a bit better."

Then he was up the steps of the companionway and Casca was hanging off the edge of the bunk, his stomach heaving, spewing nothing onto the cabin floor.

He fell back onto the bunk. Something hard but light hit him in the face, and he opened an eye to see one of the biscuits.

"Oh, Jupiter's ass," he groaned, and closed his eyes again, feeling feebly for the biscuit with his hand so that he could throw it away from him.

He found it and was about to hurl it across the cabin when it occurred to his long disciplined mind that the seaman should know what he was talking about. He had thrown the biscuits at him callously enough, but had also urged him to try them.

Shuddering, his stomach in spasm, Casca put the biscuit to his mouth. It was as hard as a plank. He tried to bite away a piece and failed. He had to clamp his teeth on a corner of the biscuit and lever with his hands to break off a piece. He closed his teeth on it and tried to chew. Some saliva ran down his throat and he felt the spasm in his gut diminish.

He chomped away at the chunk of tasteless material, feeling his stomach relax a little with each bite.

He opened his eyes, but caught sight of the wildly swinging lamp and clamped them shut again.

But he felt better. Minute by minute as he crunched his way through the biscuit his stomach calmed down. But if he opened his eyes or tried to sit up, he was instantly as sick as ever.

He laughed to himself. Had he really thought only half an hour ago that he was dying?

Two or three hours passed with Casca munching his way through one rock-hard biscuit after another. Sandy came below again and grinned at him.

"Better, eh? If you can make it to the galley, take ye a handful or two of sugar." He was gone again.

Sugar?

Casca swung his legs off the bunk—and promptly fell on his face. He lay there on the floor until the gut-wrenching spasms eased, then dragged himself to his feet and moved carefully to the galley.

He found the ship's biscuits and took a handful. There was a large wooden bin full of black sugar, and he dipped a mug full of it.

He staggered back to the bunk and lay there alternately chewing biscuits and sucking on fingers dipped in the sticky sugar.

When Sandy next appeared a couple of hours later, he was able to speak.

"Are we in a hurricane?"

The sailor shrugged. "Dunno. A hell of a dirty night, I reckon. Rudder's damn near torn off."

Then he must have slept. When he awoke the motion of the ship seemed easier, and when he went to the galley for more sugar and biscuits, Chou Lui was working over the stove.

As Casca moved he was thrown first against one side of the ship, then in a series of staggering steps, against the other. He marveled at the placid Oriental who managed, on his widespread legs, to remain in front of his cookpots, working as unconcernedly as he might have in the San Francisco restaurant he had left to join the *Rangaroa*.

When day broke Casca was awake, and he went on deck.

Ulf, the second mate, a taciturn Scandinavian, was at the helm, Sandy and an able seaman on the foredeck, the rest of the crew asleep below.

The seas were still gigantic. Enormous waves, as high as the masts of the ship, came bounding from the far horizon to lift the *Rangaroa* on their backs and surge away toward the outer edge of the boundless ocean. A white-crested monster, ten or fifteen feet taller than the rest, caught Ulf unawares, the ship answering slowly to the damaged rudder. The wave struck the side of the ship like a battering ram. Green water broke many feet deep over the deck, washing Casca into the lee scuppers.

As he regained his feet, soaked and spluttering, Ulf let out a rare, dry laugh. "She's in a hurry, that one. Left Lima yesterday, got a date in Sydney next Tuesday."

Casca shook his head in amazement. True enough, they were about halfway between Peru and Australia, with virtually nothing anywhere in between except this tiny ship to impede the regal passage of the gigantic seas.

He reflected that all of the lands he'd traveled in his immensely long life—the whole of Europe, Persia, China, and America—could all be dropped into this mighty ocean and still there would be more sea than land.

What on earth had made him come here? Never before had he experienced such seas. Had he known what a bad sailor he could be, nothing would have induced him to leave the Nevada railroad camp where he'd wound up after the defeat of the Confederate armies, driving spikes for a dollar a day.

Nothing, that is, except a corpse to explain, a pretty girl to escort, and a head full of the tales he'd heard of easy money and beautiful women in the South Pacific.

Throughout the war Sergeant Case Rafferty Lonnergan had been mightily impressed with the efficacy of railroads in moving men and materials. He was astonished at the siege of Chattanooga, when the Union Army moved twenty-three thousand men together with horses, wagons, cannon, ammunition, tents, and cookhouses from Virginia to Bridgeport, Alabama, in less than a week to rescue the besieged Union troops.

The commander-in-chief, who had made his considerable private fortune as attorney for the Illinois Central Railroad, was impressed, too, and made the man responsible—Daniel C. McCallum—a general for his achievement.

The railroad lawyer moved fast to ensure that the Union be further tied together with the steel rails, and in 1862, with the outcome of the war still very much in doubt, he signed the Pacific Railroad Act, granting charter to two new railroad companies. The Union Pacific started from Omaha, Nebraska, and moved west. The Central Pacific pushed east from Sacramento, California, over the Sierra Nevada mountains.

By 1866 the Union Pacific had reached two hundred miles west of the Missouri River. Casca's gang was camped at Plum Creek when Chief Spotted Tail and his Sioux braves derailed the supply train, scalped the crew, and looted the boxcars.

General Dodge, the Union Pacific's chief engineer, arrived to inspect the damage and was appalled at the disorderly tent city that had grown up around the construction camp. Gamblers and whiskey peddlers had almost taken over the camp. Murder and robbery were becoming commonplace.

General Dodge ordered the local boss, Jack Casement, to clean house. Casement went to each tent in the construction camp and offered pay to any man who had a gun and was willing to use it.

"What's the job?" some of the men asked.

"What's the pay?" was Casca's question.

"Five dollars for the day, and another fifty for each and every gambler and fancy man you run out of town or kill."

"How do I prove how many I've run out of town?" a young spiker asked.

"Might be hard if they ain't around," was Casement's answer.

He was careful to announce that he would not countenance murder, and that no bonus would be paid for men shot in the back or while unarmed. He pointed out that all the gamblers were professional cheats, and that where a gambler was called for cheating, any resultant dispute would be held a fair fight.

The railroad men followed his instructions, involved themselves in poker games with the gamblers, called them for cheating, and in most cases died discovering that the professional cheats were also professional gunslingers.

Casca followed the instructions to the letter.

"Hey, you cheating son of a bitch," he hollered to the first man he killed, just before he fired. The gambler, caught unawares in the camp's only street, had indeed turned to face him, and was even thinking about reaching for his derringer as Casca's .38 blew a hole through his chest.

Five more gamblers went the same way, Casca lending each of them the first one's derringer for as long as it took for the railroad marshal to arrive, inspect the corpse, and declare the fight fair.

By sunset most of the railroad men were following Casca's example, and the few gamblers left alive hurried to leave the tent city for the more hospitable desert.

A few days later General Dodge arrived and demanded a report.

"There it is." Casement pointed to a row of new graves. General Dodge nodded, and a lot of men got rich that day, including Casca.

In California the Central Pacific had been slowed by the rugged mountains and fierce storms. Construction boss Charles Crocker hired an army of Chinese laborers and set out to carve a path through the mountains, building bridges and boring tunnels on the largest scale and at the fastest pace ever attempted.

Blizzards buried the roadbed under drifts thirty to forty feet deep. Crocker built snowsheds to protect the track so that supplies could get through from Sacramento. Eventually the snowsheds covered forty miles of track.

The rails were laid at astonishing speed, four rails going down every minute. Behind the rail layers came the spikers and bolters, driving ten spikes to each rail, four hundred rails to each mile, and eighteen hundred miles to go to San Francisco. Forty carloads of rails, spikes, food, and ammunition were needed at the railhead every day to maintain the breakneck construction pace.

As they both reached Nevada the race between the two companies intensified. The railroad lawyer from Illinois had been generous to the railroad companies. Each mile of track laid was worth nearly $100,000 from the public purse and brought with it a gift of six square miles of public land. On a good day either company might lay six to eight or even ten miles of track for a gain of roughly a million dollars and sixty square miles of land, some of which was to become the most valuable land in the world.

Each company's survey team sought out its own route, and soon the two roadbeds were being laid parallel to each other.

It didn't matter a damn if the railroad never ran—the companies were making millions of dollars just laying track.

General Dodge called a stop-work meeting and paid his Union Pacific gangs to stand in the sun while he lauded "the westering spirit that is carrying us all across the continent," and explained to them that the Chinese were about to take away their jobs.

"What's the westering spirit?" Casca whispered to his shaker.

"Greed, matey, simple greed," the old man replied.

The Paddys needed no further encouragement, and attacked the Chinese with shovels and spikes and boots and fists. The Chinese cookhouses were overturned, the camps set on fire, the thoroughly terrorized Chinese fleeing into the desert.

The next day the line moved not an inch to the east and five miles to the west. The gangers collected their usual dollar each, and Union Pacific collected half a million dollars and thirty square miles of land that might have gone to its competitor.

Buffalo meat and beans were the staple diet of the Irish railroad gangs. Professional shooters with heavy muzzle-loading .50 caliber Sharps rifles could creep to within fifty yards of a grazing herd.

English tanners discovered a way to tan buffalo hides to produce much prized "Buffe" coats of the fine, soft leather for European army officers. The price of buffalo hides leaped and Casca was tempted to become a shooter.

A good shooter could down a hundred head in a morning, his skinning crew staking the hides out on the prairie to dry. A well-cured hide was worth three to four dollars.

But to Casca it was a low grade occupation—not hunting, no danger—about like being a butcher in a slaughter-house.

So he stayed at the spike and listened to the old Paddy's endless tales of easy money and beautiful women in the South Pacific.

CHAPTER TWO

Slaves.

"There's fortunes to be made in slaves for Australia, now they ain't allowed here no more," the toothless old shaker had said when Casca had lamented his poorly paid sweat for the Union Pacific Railroad.

He was working in one of the gangs of mainly Irish laborers who were pushing the iron road west a rail at a time to meet the Chinese gangs who were moving it eastward from San Francisco. His impressive physique had gotten him a job as a spike driver, and his talkative workmate's spindly frame had gotten him the job as Casca's shaker—his job being to hold the six-foot spike, try not to shake, and pray that Casca's nine-pound hammer didn't miss.

"Slaves?" Casca queried.

"Aye, sonny, slaves. Slaves for Australia. Most of my father's family were slaves there, convicts they called 'em. But snaring a hare ain't a hangin' offense no more, so they've had to stop shipping Paddys there. Anyway, Ireland's too far to go for slaves when there's plenty of 'em just offshore in Fiji."

"But isn't slavery illegal everywhere now?"

"Not at all sonny. Now that it's illegal here, the Australian plantations are producing sugar and cotton even cheaper than the South used to. Not agin slavery, are ye?"

Casca thought for an instant of his time as a slave in an Aegean copper mine, on the oar benches of a Roman galley and a Spanish galleon, and a dozen other times in his life. He thought, too, of the numbers of times he had bought slaves, conquered and enslaved whole cities, dealt in slaves, transported slaves. "I'm neither for it nor against it."

"Ain't ye a Confederate?"

Casca stopped swinging his hammer, took off his Confederate cap, and wiped the sweat from his brow.

"I wasn't fighting for slavery. I was fighting for an independent Virginia—and for pay. Better pay than I'm getting here. Better work too—shooting Yankees.

"I'm a mercenary. The definition lies in the core of the meaning of the word. You intend to come out in front financially on the deal—and alive to enjoy it. The only word for any other approach to professional warfare is idiocy."

And Casca was no idiot. If he was doomed to this damned existence forever, then he was going to come out in front all the way, all the time.

Except, as it happened, when he got drunk, or stoned, or over-ambitious, or fell in love or in lust, or simply fell. Then he'd wake up to find that he had fucked up again, that he'd lost or squandered all his money. Maybe even had to pay for the experience too.

But at least he knew what the game was about. Or that's the way it looked to him when he felt optimistic, which was most of the time.

At the other times the very idea of mercenary, or even of soldiery, was as much of a mystery as everything else he'd encountered in his first two thousand years.

"The Cannibal Isles, young fella, that's the place to be for an adventurous young pup like you. Shipping slaves to Australia, there's fortunes to be made. You take my word for it young 'un. I've been there and seen it. Don't mess with gold in California. Only bankers and saloon keepers get rich on that gold."

Well, Casca had thought, it can't be any worse than driving spikes for a dollar a day, being fed on beans, and patronized by his shaker, whom he had already outlived twenty times.

"Strange gods they have there." The toothless old man chuckled.

"Strange gods? How strange?"

He heard again the Nazarene's curse on him. For the first few hundred years Casca, hoping for an end to his life, had looked for the new Christ in Rome and Constantinople, Jerusalem and Bethlehem; and then after more than another thousand years, in the places where new Christian religions were appearing—Switzerland, Germany, and then England.

Eventually he had realized that, just as the Messiah's first coming had confused and dismayed the seers and scholars of the Jewish religion, his second coming would just as surely be a shock to the wise men of the Christian religions. So he'd looked elsewhere. In Moslem mosques, in Hindu temples, in Buddhist monasteries, amongst the pyramids of the Aztecs.

He had nothing to lose by searching the thatched temples of the South Seas. If the King of Heaven could once visit earth as a carpenter's son who wandered dusty roads in dubious company, might he not come again as a pearl diver?

"You get yourself to Fiji with just one old musket, and you can get yourself a hundred slaves in a morning's work, ship 'em to New South Wales, and you're a rich man."

"So how come you're not rich?"

"How you know I ain't?" the shaker snapped, cringing alongside the spike as Casca rained down on it with the nine-pound hammer, and the old Irishman talked on endlessly of the islands and their women and the money to be made.

Later that evening Fifi L'Amour arrived at the camp in a wagon with six girls and a piano player. Annie O'Grady, the smallest and prettiest of the girls, fell in love with Casca, and an enormous Irishman named Cassidy fell in love with her.

Casca didn't want to fight over the girl, but the Irish giant tried repeatedly to provoke him. Casca even allowed him to declaim that: "All Eyetalians is dago scum," and, "All Confederates is traitors."

Casca parried so many insults and avoided so many invitations to fight that Cassidy came to the conclusion that in spite of his build and his scars, Casca couldn't fight. Resolving to take Annie away from Casca, Cassidy arrived at Casca's tent in the middle of the night, armed with a six-foot railroad spike in case Casca gave him any trouble.

But when Cassidy tried to take the girl from Casca's bed, Cassidy realized too late that he had sadly misjudged the situation, and a fight erupted, and although Cassidy was a hulk of a man, Casca had the advantage of hundreds of years of fighting experience. He simply kicked the Irishman in the soft spot between his legs, and when the giant bent over howling, grabbing his family jewels, Casca took a wind up with his right fist, and with the bulk of his weight behind the thrust, swung a right uppercut into the man's face, making a pulp of his once prominent nose. When it was over Cassidy had three feet of a railroad spike through his gut, and Fifi's wagon hurriedly left the camp with Casca sharing the driver's seat with the piano player.

So he had set out across the deserts, passing along the way the remains of countless madmen who had dreamed of gold in California. In San Francisco he had taken passage on the *Rangaroa,* a trading schooner about to sail for the South Seas with a cargo of iron stoves, crinolines, and corsets for the port of Levuka on the island of Ovalu, the seat of government of Cakabau, king of Fiju, the most infamous of all the cannibal islands of the South Pacific and the new capital of the world's slave trade.

The *Rangaroa* was making ready to leave port when word arrived that the cook had been murdered that afternoon in an alleyway along the length of the San Francisco waterfront known as the Barbary Coast. His killer had no doubt mistaken him for a newly landed seaman with pockets full of money, rather than a destitute sailor desperate enough to ship out for the Cannibal Isles.

This piece of bad luck, together with the *Rangaroa*'s destination, made it almost impossible for the captain to hire another sea cook.

Larsen had looked at his only passenger. "Suppose I return your passage money and you ship as cook instead? I'll pay you well—if you can cook."

Casca shook his head. "Then you won't be paying me at all, I have cooked on occasion, and through extremity of hunger I have even eaten what I cooked. But I would not care to do so for the months that we will be at sea. And you would not like it either."

Larsen let out a long breath. "Can't sail without a cook. I'll just have to find one ashore somehow."

He turned to leave. At the head of the gangway he glanced back. "Care to have a last look at the town?" he asked Casca.

Casca leaped at the opportunity. He had only arrived in San Francisco the previous day, and had seen nothing of the city. He snatched up his jacket and cap and followed the captain to the pier.

They left the China Basin and walked the length of Barbary Coast waterfront, its sidewalks crowded with seamen from every race and nation on earth: tall, blue-eyed Norse men; squat, broad-nosed Balts; small, smartly dressed French matelots; neat, dark Latins off the huge Spanish and Portuguese galleys that plied from South America with their oar benches manned by convicts; groups of rollicking Irishmen out of Liverpool, shouting drunk and looking for someone to fight; and Lascars, Indians, Chinese, Negroes.

Larsen shouldered his way through the throng as if he knew where he was going, and Casca followed, wondering that this exotic city belonged to the same nation as the states of Georgia and Tennessee where he had spent the years of the recent war between the states.

Larsen knew that the Alaskan salmon season had just ended and that the city was full of Chinese cannery workers who had returned in the 'tween decks of the ships laden with the canned fish that would be re-exported from San Francisco to the world in ships such as the *Rangaroa*.

They turned away from the waterfront and Casca noticed a rapid change around him. Now the sidewalks were even more crowded, but the people were all Chinese, the men blue clad with long mustaches and pigtails; the women mincing along in tiny steps in mostly blue and black working clothes, exquisitely embroidered gowns, and now and then in brilliant yellows, greens, and reds. These brightly dressed women wore their blue-black hair in lacquered curls and were always accompanied by three or four husky young men who made way for them through the crowds.

They turned into a doorway and down a long passageway to an eating hall. Scores of Chinese working men sat on benches eating with chopsticks from large bowls in the center of each table.

Larsen found two vacant places and sat down. As Casca sat beside him, Larsen handed him a bowl then filled his own bowl with rice and some light-colored meat. Casca did the same and found the meat delicious.

"What is it?" he asked, and didn't quite catch Larsen's reply mumbled through a mouthful of food.

"Pig-aw-gun? What's that in English?"

"That is English. Pig organ. An organ of a pig."

Casca studied the meat. "Which organ?"

Larsen laughed. "From the point of view of the pig, I guess you'd say his vital organ."

Casca stopped chewing for a moment while he thought over this information.

"Eat up," said Larsen. "You won't see fresh meat again for a month."

A busboy came to the table to clear away used dishes, and Larsen spoke to him.

"Savvy English?"

"Oh, yes, savvy English, work English ships."

"Aha!" Larsen was delighted. "You cook?"

"Oh, yes, Chou Lui cook on ships Shanghai, Madras, London, New York, Rio, Santiago, San Francisco."

"You work my ship to Sydney, Australia?"

The Chinese raised his eyebrows. "Australia? How much pay?"

"Twenty dollars Tahiti, forty more dollars Sydney."

"How much profit share?"

"Half of one percent."

"When sail?"

"One hour."

"Okay. Wait please."

He moved to another table, and then another and another, scooping up the used utensils and chopsticks and carrying piles of bowls higher than his head to the kitchen at the back of the room.

He returned from the kitchen without his apron, shrugging into a black embroidered jacket.

"Ah, very good, we go now."

He led them through a maze of narrow streets, alleys, and stairways and asked them to wait outside a tall, narrow building which housed a Chinese apothecary on the ground floor. While they waited Casca studied the platters of dried sea horses, deer antlers, shark fins, ginseng roots, and other Chinese medicines.

In a few minutes Chou Lui reappeared toting a small duffel bag, and within the hour the *Rangaroa*'s crew were letting go the lines and Casca was watching the city of San Francisco slip out of sight into its mantle of fog.

As they cleared the heads of the Golden Gate to the Pacific Ocean Larsen handed the helm over to Sandy.

"Just keep her out of the potato patch," Larsen said, laughing.

"You can count on that," the Scot replied as he took control.

"Potato patch?" Casca queried.

Sandy jerked his head toward where Casca could see waves breaking on rocks.

"Between us and them breakers there's rocks lurking just under the water. They've ripped the bottoms out of so many ships the local seamen say the waves are sown with their potatoes." He gestured toward the many sacks on *Rangaroa*'s deck. "I sure don't intend to add our spuds to the crop."

"I should think not," bellowed a cheerful Irish voice, and a red head came from the companionway. "Even a sassencah Scot would rather eat a spud than sow it in the sea." The head was followed by a muscular body.

"And only an Irish bog trotter like Liam O'Dwyer would talk such nonsense," said Sandy by way of introduction. "Mister Case Lonnergan, meet the bosun of the ship."

"A name from the auld sod I'm thinking," said Liam as they shook hands, "but you don't look Irish."

"What is in a look or name these days, what with all the traveling and cross-breedin' people do. Let's just say the name has served me well enough and let it go at that, but if you wish, you can call me by another name I've not heard for a long time. Casca!"

He didn't know why he gave his true name, but it was done and he liked the sound of it. He had carried too many others over the long years, and on this lonely ship heading to the edge of the world it was not likely that it would do him any harm.

"Well, then," said the Scot, "we'll call ye Casca, as you're leaving the states and save ye the indignity of carrying an Irish name any farther."

"In the name of Jesus," Liam shouted in feigned anger, "give me strength not to strangle this idiot who doesn't even know that his own name comes from Ireland in the first place."

Sandy laughed. "Oh, we're not so ignorant. We know where we came from, but we prefer not to think about it."

"Well," said Casca, "if it's all right with you warring Gaels, I'll accept Casca and keep Rafferty Lonnergan. The name got me a job with the Paddys on the railroad, and a few of them weren't such bad guys—for barbarians."

Over the next several weeks Casca got to know all the crew. The first watch of the day was run by Weston, a

burly New Englander who was at the helm from midnight.
On a thong around his thick, sunburned neck he wore the
largest shark's tooth Casca had ever seen. At four Weston
was relieved by Ulf, and at eight Liam took over. There
were also an able seaman and an ordinary seaman on each
watch to handle the sails and keep lookout, and for company for the helmsman. *Rangaroa* was a working merchant
ship, and the officer of the watch ran the ship most of the
time from the helm, the two seamen on the foredeck ready
to take his orders or relieve him as required.

There was not much for them to do. *Rangaroa* was on a
broad reach, the northwesterly breezes coming over her
starboard side, keeping her nicely heeled to port as she
kept her heading of 165, bound for the islands of Tahiti.

CHAPTER THREE

Day after day, night after night, week after week the *Rangaroa* bounded through the seas, and Casca enjoyed the voyage more and more. They passed to the southeast of Hawaii and picked up the northeast trades, replacing the northwesterly winds. *Rangaroa* changed tack and now lay over on her starboard side, running before the steady breeze, making good time with all sails set.

They crossed the equator with a great deal of tomfoolery, Casca being the butt of numerous pranks according to custom, since he was the only passenger aboard and claimed to have never previously ventured into the southern half of the planet. His head was ceremonially shaved; he was thrown into the sea in a harness on the end of a line. The idea was to drag him a little way behind the ship, but they were in the doldrums, becalmed between the northeast and the southeast trades.

Casca swam around for a while in the warm water, enjoying himself immensely. Had he known seagoing was so much fun, he would have taken to it much earlier in his long life.

Sandy dressed up as a girl, in a series of outfits borrowed from the ship's cargo. First he appeared in an elegant crinoline, then in a skirt made of sailcloth, a striped sailor's jersey stuffed with two potatoes, and a wig made from teased-out threads of rope. Chou Lui produced a box of Chinese paint colors and rouged his cheeks, blackened his eyelashes, painted shadows around his eyes, reddened his lips. With his small frame he looked and acted a very pretty little slut, playing the part thoroughly, dancing and flirting outrageously with all the crew, stripping lasciviously to a corset.

Rangaroa flopped around on the flat sea for several more days, the sails hanging useless from the gaffs, the helmsmen striving hour after hour to maneuver the ship to catch the breath of any vagrant breeze. The whole crew, including Chou Lui, and even Casca, took turns at the helm.

At noon each day Larsen took a sextant shot, calculated the ship's position and recorded it on the chart and in the log. Some days they made as little as ten miles, and these miles were hard won, each helmsman in turn coaxing every possible mile from the almost nonexistent wind, trying to inch the ship toward where they might pick up the southeast trades.

One night when Casca was at the helm he allowed his attention to wander. The sails fell slack as the wind shifted slightly. Casca didn't notice and failed to adjust the heading, and the sails flapped across to the other tack.

Several seamen were on deck and they sprang to the ropes, but there was not enough wind to move the yards and they could not bring the ship back on to course. Weston motioned to Casca to put the helm over, and they swung a great arc all the way around the compass to regain their course.

When Larsen did his noon sight they had lost three miles for the day. Casca was profoundly depressed, but all the others, even Ulf, made light of it.

"It don't really make no blamed difference," he said, "we'll make up three miles in twenty minutes when we get a good blow."

Maybe, Casca thought, but I've still cost the ship a whole day's work.

The next night during Weston's watch, Casca tried another trick at the helm. This time he was determined at all costs to ensure that the ship would gain some miles, and certainly not lose any.

He kept his attention concentrated entirely on the sails, striving every moment to lay the ship into the path of even the faintest breeze, struggling to keep the canvas filled with the very light air.

He was vaguely aware of the movements of the sailors on the foredeck. The able seamen had been sent below to repair sail, since they were not needed on deck, and the mate and Sandy were forward of the fore cabin skylight, out of Casca's view.

Faint sounds from this direction obtruded into Casca's awareness and he resolutely shut them out as he listened for the faint flutter of the sail that would warn him of the danger of the canvas being backwinded, repeating his error of the previous night.

Gradually he became aware that the sounds from the foredeck were like those of a scuffle, and he called out, "You guys all right there?"

There was no answer, and the scuffling sounds increased. He thought he heard Sandy's muffled voice.

"Sandy?" he called.

"Mind your own fuckin' business," Weston's voice came back to him, and again some faint undistinguishable noises from Sandy.

"What's going on?" Casca demanded.

There was no reply, but the sounds were now unmistakable. Weston and Sandy were wrestling on the deck.

For just a moment Casca hesitated. Perhaps it was none of his business. He knew that if he left the helm for a second, the ship could lose again every mile that the crew had sweated for in the past twenty-four hours. On the other hand Sandy was a friend and the sounds were disturbing.

He hesitated for one more instant, thinking, If nothing is really amiss how the hell will I explain the fuck-up to the crew? Then there was a muffled yelp of pain from Sandy and he dropped the helm and ran forward.

Just beyond the skylight Weston had Sandy pinned face

down on the deck, one hand clamping a length of hemp into his mouth, the other hand tugging down the boy's pants. Weston's pants were already down around his ankles, his legs a mass of thick, black hair.

Casca yelled as he ran toward the struggling pair.

"Fuck off, passenger," Weston grunted, and tried once more to force his entry into Sandy's struggling body.

With the skill learned in a thousand fights, and the strength of endless centuries of physical training and hard work, Casca chopped with the heel of his hand at the mate's thick, hairy neck.

Weston's powerful body jerked spasmodically in momentary paralysis and he released his hold on the boy. Sandy wriggled away as Casca seized the mate's thick neck in one powerful hand and smashed his face into the deck. He was repeating the movement for the third or fourth time when he heard the flutter of the sails.

Sandy was now on his feet, crying in rage, pain, and humiliation and tugging up his trousers. Casca drove the mate's nose once more into the deck and raced aft for the helm.

Too late.

The sails came across to the wrong side, and the *Rangaroa* was heading ninety degrees away from their desired course. Sandy ran to the foresail and handed it across the deck, tugging it through the resistance of the light breeze. But the four sails on the two masts remained obstinately backwinded.

Casca cursed. Without more men to hand across the sails, it was hopeless to try to regain the tack. But to call the crew would expose Sandy's embarrassment, and Casca knew that the boy would rather go over the side.

To put the helm over and make the necessary full circle of the compass would also alert everybody below decks, yet every second the ship was being carried farther from its course.

Casca was saved any further thinking about the problem by the appearance before him of Weston with a belaying pin in his hand, and the heavy pin was moving fast for Casca's head.

He threw himself across the deck, putting the helm hard over, dodging the heavy blow, to fall sprawling by the starboard rail. The burly mate was after him, the pin upraised for another blow.

But the blow never came. With all the power of his massive legs, Casca came up from the deck in a great rush and met Weston halfway, one powerful hand grabbing Weston's wrist. There was a sharp crack, and a hideous scream from the mate as Casca's single-handed grip broke his wrist.

Thoroughly enraged, Casca chopped again at Weston's neck, and the mate sagged unconscious to the deck as the alerted crew came running up the companionway.

"Get away forward," he snapped, and Sandy ran for the flapping foresail.

Ulf was the first man to reach the deck, and he ran for the helm.

"Give it to me," he shouted, and Casca was happy to oblige.

"Get 'em over boys," Ulf shouted to the crew, and they manhandled the sails across the decks, holding them against the breeze on the port tack while Ulf gently moved the tiller about, seeking that magic spot that would fill the canvas.

The man had been born on a fishing smack in a storm in the middle of winter off the coast of Greenland—nothing special in the lives of his mother and father, who had both similarly been born aboard their parents' fishing boats. From arctic gale to tropic doldrum there was not a wind or a sea on the planet that Ulf didn't know and couldn't master.

One degree at a time, one second of one degree at a time, he brought the reluctant ship about, coaxing it into the wind so that the light breeze bellied the sails.

Larsen had arrived on deck with everybody else, but was forward with the rest of the crew, handling sail like an ordinary seaman while his second mate's skill saved the precious miles of the day's sailing.

The sails filled, the topsails came across, and *Rangaroa* was again moving serenely into the wind.

Larsen came aft to where Weston lay on the deck. He guessed easily enough what had happened, and asked no embarrassing questions, but gestured to two seamen.

"Get this garbage below," he snapped, and they lifted the mate and carried him down the companionway.

A little later in the night Larsen spoke to Casca. "I've had a look at Weston's arm. What did you use on him?"

Casca grunted. "Only my hands. His arm's broken, I suppose."

"Like it was snapped in a vise."

"Well, he asked for it."

"I don't doubt it. The man's a pig. I'm ashamed I made the mistake of hiring him. But his arm's a rare mess. You don't know as much about fixing as you do about breaking by any chance?"

"Yeah, as a matter of fact, I do."

"Well, would you have a look at it? It's beyond me. I can hack off the whole mess, of course, but I'm reluctant to take a man's hand."

"It might be a mistake not to with this one, but I'll look at it anyway. I can use the practice."

He went to where Weston lay in agony in the first mate's small cabin. He was now rotten drunk with the rum Larsen had provided to ease his pain. But he recognized Casca and cringed away from him, then became quarrelsome when he realized that he was not going to be harmed.

"Shut up or I'll snap the other one off too," Casca snarled, and the burly mate became once more a pathetic, moaning bundle of pain.

Casca gathered some small pieces of wood and some bandages. Then he got two seamen to hoist the moaning mate into a sitting position and to hold him there.

With one swift chop of his hand Casca rendered Weston unconscious. He grabbed his hand and deftly jerked it, to straighten as well as possible the mess of smashed bones, then splinted and wrapped it securely before consciousness returned to Weston.

"Better than a bastard like you deserves," Larsen commented as he handed the rum bottle to the awakening man. "Thank the man for your hand, you bum, I'd have taken it off."

Weston put on a disgusting performance of grabbing the bottle, gulping rum, dribbling, crying, cringing, slobbering thanks and apologies, before slumping once more into a drunken stupor.

CHAPTER FOUR

Light winds stayed with them all the way to Tahiti, and Casca discovered another aspect of sailing in the tropics. Broiling sun burned down relentlessly out of a cloudless, bright-blue sky. The sea was a vast, flat, shimmering mirror of silver blue. The *Rangaroa* wallowed along, barely making steerage way, rolling and pitching until Casca's stomach shook and he felt queasy.

The crew grew daily more restive and querulous. The ill-natured Weston had been ·dismissed from duty, and the captain now stood his watch. Weston spent most of the sweltering days below in his cabin, occasionally coming on deck in the middle of the night. He ate alone and didn't speak to anyone.

One morning he was missing, and the shark's tooth hung on Sandy's chest. Larsen, who had kept the log blank, now brought it up to date, recording Weston as lost overboard and not mentioning anything of his offense or the fight with Casca.

One soft, moonlit night the lookout cried, "Land ho," and everybody raced onto deck.

Far off on the horizon a shapeless blur like a low cloud could be seen against the sky. Larsen nodded happily.

"Yeah, looks like land, for sure. Just keep your heading and call me if it moves." He went back to his bunk.

"If it moves?" Casca queried the helmsman.

He grinned. "These are strange waters. Things are often not what they seem. Could be a cloud, could be nothing. Your eyes can play tricks on you in these latitudes."

Casca stayed on deck, enthralled at the mystery of the distant island. And so it proved to be, growing larger and larger as the hours passed.

But after a little Casca began to believe his eyes were indeed playing tricks on him. The island took on the shape of a voluptuous woman lying gracefully on her back, her legs spread, knees pointing to the sky.

He shook his head, but the vision persisted.

Liam was now at the helm and he grinned at Casca.

"What do you see?"

"Well, I suppose it is an island, but . . ."

"A promising-looking island, wouldn't you say?"

Casca laughed. "So, it looks the same to you? I'm glad to hear it. Thought maybe I was going crazy."

"It's Hua Wahine," the Irishman said. "In the ugly language of the barbarians across the Irish Sea, those lovely words translate into 'woman's cunt'."

"Mmm," Casca mused, "I like Hua Wahine."

Once ashore he like the island even better. It was an island that kept its promise. The women, wahines in the local language, were plump, with wide, long thighs and shapely, short lower legs; they had lustrous black hair that reached to their waists, large dark eyes, fine, turned-up noses, wide mouths, prognathous chins.

The French soldiers and civil servants who controlled the island considered them ugly. The French missionaries, who were kept busy destroying their temples and trying to persuade these women to cover their breasts, considered them to be hopelessly depraved.

At first sight Casca was not sure whether he considered them beautiful or hideous. He quickly made up his mind and found them the most delightful women he had met in his life—lovely to look at, lighthearted, fun loving, playfully amorous.

They were welcomed into a village of thatch-roofed

bamboo huts built around a wide open space entirely
shaded by a single great teak tree.

There was a great chief's house—one enormous, open
room without walls. The floor was of millions of tiny white
beach pebbles, and the columns that held up the great
thatched roof were whole trees stripped of their bark and
elaborately carved and painted. Other trees, similarly deco-
rated, formed the roof trusses that spanned an open space
as wide as a European cathedral.

At one corner of the village there was a roofless stone
temple containing a number of gigantic gods carved of
stone, the biggest sculptures Casca had ever seen. But nowhere near the village, nor anywhere else that he traveled
about the island, did Casca see such stones, or even stones
of the size used for the temple walls. It was clear that it
would take many men to lift even the smallest of these.
The huge stone gods could not possibly have been moved
without either horses or elephants.

Or, perhaps, steam engines. But neither horses nor elephants, nor engines of any kind had ever been seen on the
island.

"Their ancestors built the temples," Larsen told him in
reply to his questions.

"But how?"

"There is no explanation," Larsen replied. "Take my
word for it. In a lifetime of questions and investigation you
will get no closer to the secret. There is simply no explanation."

Casca shrugged. One more unexplainable mystery
meant nothing to him. He went back to enjoying the local
women, the fruits that fell ripe from breadfruit and mango
and papaya and coconut trees, and the fish and crabs and
lobster and turtles that the ocean provided in return for only
the slightest effort.

He spent each of their three nights ashore with a different young girl. He would have been content with the first
one, or the second, but it seemed that the girls themselves
preferred to rotate amongst the crew.

When they talked enthusiastically of the children that

they might procreate, he found it necessary to lie to them —recalling that afternoon when, startled by the voice from the cross, he had wiped his hand across his face. A few drops of the tortured preacher's blood had run down the haft of his spear and onto his hand, and when they touched his lips his body was seized in convulsions that threw him to the ground at the foot of the cross. From that day his own blood had been poisonous, his sperm lifeless.

He had never sired a child and knew that he never would, but he promised each girl a beautiful blue-eyed babe, and wished in his heart that it could be true.

As the *Rangaroa* prepared to sail, Casca and the whole crew were unhappy to be leaving this land where music and love and laughter never stopped, but they reassured each other that they would be just as pleasantly welcomed in Fiji.

"But surely the Fijians are cannibals?" he said.

"That they are," was the reply, "and the hungriest, if not quite the fiercest, cannibals in the whole Pacific—and the friendliest, funniest bunch of fuckers on the face of the earth."

"Eating people isn't funny," Casca said.

"Ah," Sandy answered, "for the Fijians everything is funny, even hurricanes and earthquakes. And a dead man is only a piece of meat when all is said and done, and if he ain't eaten, he'll only go rotten. There's no other meat in these parts, do you see?"

"Then why aren't the Tahitians cannibals?" he asked.

Everybody on deck laughed.

"But of course they are," Liam told him. "You don't see it every day, and no more you will in Fiji, but all the people of the Pacific eat people."

Casca thought of the three lovely, soft, feminine bodies that he'd held in his arms, of their gentle nature, sweet smiles, and affectionate lovemaking. It was hard to believe that these delightful creatures were greedy, bloodthirsty cannibals. He privately decided that the crew was joshing him, that it couldn't be so.

"We're going to be in Fiji for weeks," Liam said, "so you'll be sure to see some cannibal feasts."

Ulf broke out laughing, an event so rare that everybody looked at him.

"You might see it sooner," he spluttered through his laughter, "lookee, here comes the new hand."

Larsen was still ashore, seeking to hire a man to make up the crew shortage, and now he was approaching the ship, accompanied by a huge black man carrying a great, carved chest on one shoulder. Larsen was a big man, but his companion was much bigger.

Casca had never seen a man like him. His great mop of jet-black hair was like that of some Africans, but thicker, longer, and stronger. The face had high-set cheekbones, a finely chiseled nose and chin, a wide, generously lipped mouth, and eyes set wide apart in deep sockets. Features almost like a black European, Casca thought.

As the two men came aboard Casca saw that, in fact, the man was not black, but a deep, coppery brown like the stock of an old musket.

"Meet the new bosun," Larsen said as he came aboard. "Foster," he continued to an able seaman, "show the bosun around will you?" He hurried away to attend to his many concerns.

Foster came from Charleston, South Carolina, and before the Civil War his parents had owned a few slaves. He was not impressed with the idea of working under a black bosun.

"What about Liam?" he asked after Larsen.

"He's new second mate," Larsen threw over his shoulder as he descended the companionway, "and Ulf's mate."

The seamen on deck let out a cheer. Liam did a little comic jig, and Ulf smiled. Born at sea, he had started work on his father's boat at four, and it had taken forty-three more years to make it to the rank of first mate.

"So what are ye all waiting for?" he snapped at his crew, "we'll never clear port if you lazy bums don't shift your asses."

They moved quickly to ready the ship for sea.

"He's a glum son of a bitch," the irrepressible Sandy chuckled when they were safely forward, "but he's probably the best damn seaman on the planet."

There was a small chorus of ayes from the other sailors.

In the stern Ulf turned to the Fijian, who was grinning hugely and smiled even wider when Ulf pointed to the companionway.

"You'll find another heathen in the galley," Ulf said. "He'll break out some blankets for ye."

"Yes, sir," the Fijian grinned, "but Kini not heathen. I'm Christian."

"The hell you are," Ulf snorted. "Christians are white." He turned away to his duties, and Kini went below to the galley.

CHAPTER FIVE

The fine weather and light winds carried them into the Koro Sea, a small, island-fringed sea about the size of what European sailors call the Great North Sea, set within the planet-reaching proportions of the mighty Pacific. It was here they had run into the violent storm that nearly finished them off.

The storm had lasted for several days and nights, and now it seemed they were coming out of it. The seas were growing calmer by the hour, the wind now a steady, heavy blow, a good, roaring, following wind to sail with.

The damaged *Rangaroa* was way off course, somewhere south southwest of the fabled Fiji islands, discovered and named the Cannibal Isles by Captain Bligh on his way back to England after the *Bounty* mutineers had set him adrift in an open boat without charts or compass.

The British had ignored the Cannibal Isles until 1860, when they were annexed by the governor of New South Wales, Sir Hercules Robinson. Fiji then became nominally a British colony. But in fact it was the possession of the Australian descendants of the gang of military criminals who had stolen that huge island out of the real sovereignty of the British Empire by yet another mutiny against the same Bligh, when he was governor of the Australian penal colony.

With the end of slavery in the United States in the wake of the Civil War, the small clique that owned most of Australia saw the opportunity to further enrich themselves. By using slaves from the South Pacific islands, they grew sugar and cotton more cheaply than could be matched elsewhere in the world.

A gang of missionary traders armed Cakabau, the chief of the tiny ninety-acre island of Bau, and declared him king of Fiji. Cakabau then gratefully ceded the whole of Fiji to Britain, and Sir Hercules Robinson and the Whitehall government obligingly ratified the deal, legitimatizing the reign of the bloodthirsty cannibal chief. By 1867 his regime had become infamous for the killing and eating of his subjects and the enslavement of those whom he was too sated to eat.

The *Rangaroa* was carrying cargo for Levuka, the cannibal monarch's capital, and Larsen knew that it was safe to put into port there. There was no telling just what sort of reception they might get on any of the other Cannibal Isles.

But just now there was no telling where any such island might be.

Studying the navigation chart, Larsen looked irritable, and at the same time amused. "Look at this, will you?" he said, pounding the chart with a finger as thick as a small belaying pin. "It says here: 'Some reports of a small group of islands in this vicinity.' For Christ's sake, what sort of sailing direction do ye call that?"

"Things is different in these parts," said Liam, who was studying the chart with him. "It was around these parts that Gulliver discovered Brobdignag, and not too far away he found Lilliput."

He spoke matter-of-factly, as if he would not be at all surprised to glance out the porthole and see a man standing in the sea and towering over the schooner, or another only a few inches tall, dancing on the head of a belaying pin.

"Bah, fairy tales," snorted Ulf. "Ships have gone looking for dose islands and found nutting. Just fairy tales."

"Fiction anyway," said Larsen. "I've read Swift's book."

"Have ye now?" Liam chuckled. "Then read this." He laid on the chart table an open copy of the *Pacific Islands Pilot* of 1864. "These reports is not from a dotty old Irish priest like Swift, but from hard-nosed English insurance men."

Larsen picked up the book and read: "Lloyd's agent reported hereabouts the island of Tanakuvi, longitude 172 49 West and latitude 19 36 South. But HMS *Vengeance*, searching for the island, reported depth of fifty-seven fathoms."

Larsen slammed the book shut. "It's enough to make you believe in the devil himself."

"Then you're learning something at last," chuckled Liam, ducking as Larsen playfully swung a great fist near his nose.

"There's been islands appearing and disappearing in these parts ever since Magellan found the Tuamotus four hundred years ago." Ulf chuckled drily.

"The question is," Larsen said, "what is here now? This chart is no bloody help at all. There's a ship lost every week running into uncharted islands hereabout, and I don't intend for *Rangaroa* to be another one."

Liam opened the well-thumbed copy of the *Pacific Islands Pilot* and read: "In this vicinity the *Clara Bella* reported rocks in 1836, and the *Coyne* reported a group of small islands in 1842. However, in 1849 the *Carl Gustaf* found a depth of fifty-six fathoms."

"So?" the captain queried.

Liam closed the book and slammed it on the chart table in disgust. "That's all. Not another word."

"Jesus!" Larsen shouted.

"Land ho," came a hail from the deck, and everybody scrambled for the companionway.

This time there was no doubt. The island was very clear on the horizon. Larsen looked at Sandy, who was on watch.

"How long has that been there?"

The Scot grimaced and shook his head.

"Just now, skipper. Just now. Even clear air hides things here, dammit."

Larsen looked up at the bright, cloudless sky, then back at the island and shook his head.

"Well, thank God, we saw it anyway. Let's get these sails down. There's sure to be a reef somewhere between us and the island." He shouted to the man out on the bowsprit. "How's the water?"

"Deep and clear," the seaman shouted back.

Under reduced sail the *Rangaroa* slowly approached the island. Larsen paced the deck restlessly. The whole crew was on the lookout—on the bowsprit, in the crow's nest, all over the rigging.

The man on the bowsprit called, "Changing water."

"Ready anchor," Larsen shouted, and the crew sprang to ready the forward anchor as Larsen himself went out onto the bowsprit.

Casca was as far forward as he could get without getting in the way of the crew, and he could see that the water had changed from deep blue to a dark green. As he watched it changed again, to a lighter green.

"Ready about, anchor over," Larsen shouted from the bowsprit, and came running back to the helm. The crew hefted the heavy anchor over the side and it hung there ready to drop.

Now Casca could see faint ripples ahead of the ship where an underwater reef disturbed the movement of the sea.

"Lee ho," Larsen shouted, and Sandy put the helm over. The sailors on the port side let go the ropes they were holding, and those on the starboard side hauled on theirs while others ran across the deck helping the light breeze move the sails to the other tack.

The *Rangaroa* came slowly around and the island was astern.

"Sail ho," one of the seamen shouted as he saw a boat put out from the distant island.

Soon they could see canoes coming from several points: sail canoes—two and three hulls lashed together with great, broad decks between and enormous triangular sails; single outrigger sail canoes—the outrigger a deftly shaped log, the canoe itself dug out of a log; and huge dugout canoes with twenty men at the paddles. The dugouts came racing through the water, passing the sail craft, the crews singing lustily in time with their strokes.

And rafts. Rafts of bamboo poles lashed together with vines, a single, small sail on a short mast. These came out over the reef to the *Rangaroa* and surrounded her, their smiling crews shouting welcomes.

"*Haere mai, haere mai, Valangi. Bula, bula*. Welcome, *Valangi*, welcome. Bienvenidos," and some other words in Chinese and Japanese, or perhaps Malay. They shouted welcome in all the languages they knew.

"*Valangi*," Sandy explained, "means men from the sky." He jerked his head upward toward several seamen sitting in the crosstrees. "Looks to them like we climb down the masts out of the sky."

The islanders pointed to where the other craft were coming through the unseen opening in the reef.

Larsen glanced at Ulf. "The reef might be tricky, but we'll be a damn sight safer, inside than out here. We can't sail farther till we repair the rudder anyway."

All right with me, thought Casca, who had already decided that he would feel more comfortable with the reef between him and the Pacific, rather than riding between the Pacific and the reef. "Yeah," he said, "I'll be happy to be inside the reef."

"Unless they decide to eat us," the dour Greenlander muttered flatly, giving Casca something to think about.

These people were very different from those they had left in Tahiti. They were darker, almost black, like Kini, but they wore their hair in great crinkly mops, as he did.

The first of the canoes had now reached the *Rangaroa*, and Larsen signaled to them that he would follow them back through the opening.

In a moment the crew had again shaken out *Rangaroa*'s sails, and she was under way, guided by the flotilla of rafts that took up position between the ship and the reef, shepherding her to the opening, where canoes were coming out. Just beyond the rafts Casca could see the outline of coral rocks beneath the surface.

As the ship came to the opening in the reef the wind suddenly died.

"On the fucking doorstep, like always," Larsen shouted as he put the helm up, the ship responding slowly to the torn and splintered rudder.

"Like fuckin' always," Sandy yelled as he raced forward to hand the foresail across the foredeck.

All over the deck crewmen were handling rope and hauling sail as they sought to change tack in the suddenly slackened breeze, moving the sails to use what wind there might be to keep the ship clear of the coral.

The foresail filled in the light wind, the other sails bellied slightly, and the *Rangaroa* veered away from the hacksaw teeth of the reef.

Lines of intertwined vines were passed aboard and bent together with ropes on the *Rangaroa*'s deck, and first one then several of the twenty-man canoes took up the tow, hauling the ship through the reef opening and into the safe waters of the lagoon.

As they glided through the reef Casca could see the jagged coral only yards away from the side of the *Rangaroa*. Then they were inside.

In deep, calm water Larsen let go of the helm and Sandy dropped the slack end of the foresail sheet. Seamen were furling sail, and all over the deck the crew were belaying rope. The anchor chain ran out into the bottomless well of the old volcanic crater that formed the harbor.

Casca could see the hook dangling fathoms below, but nowhere near the bottom.

It was just sunset, and now a faint offshore breeze came to them, carrying with it the scent of frangipani blossoms. Casca felt very much at ease.

He looked at the others. They were smiling. He took a deep breath of the perfume-laden air. And he smiled.

Larsen addressed his crew on the deck. "There's no way to guess what we might be heading into here. Kini tells me he doesn't know these people, but they seem as friendly as Fijians—might be as bloodthirsty too. So keep your knives handy but out of sight. Steel is unknown in thcse parts, and I'll maroon any man who gives a girl his knife to play with."

"Not what I had in mind at all." Casca laughed as he patted his knife, concealed in its sheath in his inner jacket pocket. He wondered if Larsen had a revolver somewhere about him as he felt the weight of his own .38 and its shells in his jacket pockets.

He took a deep breath of the flower-scented air. And he smiled—a big, toothy smile.

CHAPTER SIX

Canoes ferried them to the beach, where they were greeted by music and bare-breasted girls in grass skirts whose dancing was quite different from the Tahitians. The music came from wooden drums and an instrument made from a coconut half strung with strings of gut. Casca reflected that there were no animals in these islands, and forebore thinking further about just what gut might have been used.

They were taken to a fortified village on a hilltop some distance from the beach.

Casca was impressed by the village defenses. A six-foot palisade of sharpened poles leaned outward so that it was virtually unscalable by attackers. On the inside there were two horizontal rails that enabled the defenders to take up positions of advantage. There were small openings that a man had to bend double to get through. There were three of these fences to be passed through before they reached the village, a collection of thatched huts around an open space. The huts were similar to those on Hua Wahine, but these had walls of woven coconut fronds and floors of crushed seashells.

The hut they were led to was many times the size of any of the others. At the far end of the one enormous room a huge man sat cross-legged on a raised dais of coconut logs covered with seashells and grass mats. He was, perhaps, the biggest man Casca had ever seen.

He recalled that legend amongst European sailors had it that these cannibals continued to grow throughout their lives, and looking at Semele, Casca could believe it.

The man was enormous, but not in any one place. His body was one firm, muscular ball. Nowhere were there any folds of loose fat or sagging flesh. His huge head sat on a columnar neck atop a body that was as thick through from breastbone to spine as it was from shoulder to shoulder. Arms the size of Casca's legs were complemented by great legs and huge feet.

Yet when Semele moved, Casca was amazed to see that he moved easily and even gracefully.

The house filled up with people and Casca guessed that everybody in the village was there. Semele came down from the dais which Casca assumed was his private space. Not very private, he thought, and not much space either.

Everybody sat cross-legged on the floor and two women carried in a carved bowl filled with a muddy liquid. They placed it on the floor and another old man, not quite as huge as Semele, carried from it a huge whale's tooth on a rope of plaited vines, placing it at Semele's feet.

"Kava," Sandy told Casca. "They like it better than whiskey."

A glance was enough to convince Casca that he was much more likely to prefer whiskey.

The old man, Mbolo, intoned a long speech which was presumably a welcome. A younger man scooped some of the kava in a bowl made from a polished half coconut shell and with much ceremony carried it respectfully to the chief. Semele clapped his hands, then accepted the bowl and drained it, clapped three more times, said *"matha,"* returned the bowl to the young man, and everybody in the room clapped three times.

The whale's tooth, called a *tabua*, was moved to Larsen's feet, and the next bowl came to Larsen, who repeated the chief's actions. The bowl passed back and forth, going now to Mbolo and then to Casca, although the *tabua* remained by Larsen.

Casca chuckled to himself as he realized that the islanders placed him number two in the ship's company. Guess they've never heard of a passenger, he mused. He was disagreeably surprised to find that the liquid tasted every bit as bad as it looked, the only effect being a numb feeling in his tongue and gums. The bowl passed back and forth, going now to one of the islanders, then to one of the company from the *Rangaroa*.

When all the company had drunk from the bowl it continued to pass, but conversation broke out throughout the room. The language was musical, stately, and interspersed with much laughter.

The chief and those around him, to Casca's astonishment, spoke English, and reasonably good English.

Semele explained that the South Seas trader, Clevinger, had once had a post on the island and had gone to some pains to teach the villagers English.

The chief told them that this was the island of Navola Levu and that they were in the principal village, Navola. He asked many questions of Larsen and of others in the crew: where they had come from, how many days they had been at sea, and where they were bound for. His curiosity seemed endless.

After some hours of this conversation and many, many bowls of kava, a number of women entered the house, carrying banana-leaf platters laden with steaming fish, cooked bananas, papayas, breadfruit, yams, cassava, taro, and a dozen other fruits and vegetables Casca couldn't identify. The chief seemed to have an unlimited appetite, and Casca noticed that each time he reached for food, everybody did the same.

"If I'm here for long, I'll wind up as big as he is," Casca whispered to Larsen.

The chief seemed to arrive at somewhat the same thought, and singled Casca out for special questioning, apparently because he was the most powerfully built of the ship's company.

Gradually Casca became aware of a frown of puzzlement growing on the old chief's brow. A skilled interrogator himself, and the survivor of countless interrogations under all sorts of tortures, Casca realized that this quiet, casual questioner had plied him with such a complex skein of questions that he had tripped up here and there, and the wise old man had realized that there was more to Casca's past than he was prepared to relate.

Casca was surprised to find that he'd fallen into some carefully set traps in the old man's questions, more surprised still at the subtlety of the process. He was also pretty worried. He knew only too well that people do not lie without reason, and now that the chief had realized he was lying, he would surely start questing for the reason.

There was no reason other than the impossibility of explaining the truth, but suspicion would cast a cloud over the entire crew of the *Rangaroa*.

At the next question Casca fell back on a device that he had often found of use—the truth. Or part of it.

"Forgive me, Semele, but as you see, I am not one of the ship's crew, and I have a confusing history. I am a professional warrior and I have lived longer than my years indicate. I do not wish to deceive you, for I am an honest man, but it is not possible for me to explain more."

Semele nodded several times, then smiled and turned his questioning to Sandy. Casca breathed a long sigh of relief.

Gradually Casca realized that the men sitting around them were being replaced by women, and lovely young women at that. He looked around and saw that each crewman had two or three lovelies sitting near him and concentrating on him, smiling, occasionally saying some small thing in their own language, now and again a single word of English.

There were three such women next to him, and as the evening went on he discerned that there was some sort of unperceived competition going on amongst them, the one who told him her name was Alesia seemingly winning.

Casca couldn't tell how it happened, but eventually

there was only Alesia, the other women having tactfully withdrawn. People were leaving the house without any special ceremony, and Casca found himself being led away by Alesia.

She took him to a small thatched hut and lay down with him on a grass mat.

Just before dawn the next morning she woke him. It seemed to Casca they had made love just about all night and now it seemed she wanted to do so again. Very pleasant, and very flattering, but Casca wanted to sleep.

Alesia very gently but insistently maneuvered him awake and into her arms. The intensity of her passion completely overwhelmed Casca, and when it was over he was puzzled by the fierce, hungry energy of her last kiss as she leaped to her feet and ran from the hut.

For a moment Casca thought of running after her, but sexually oversated, overfed, and still, it seemed, somehow affected by the kava, he fell back into a deep sleep.

CHAPTER SEVEN

When he awoke much later in the morning he went in search of Alesia and found her at the chief's house. There, together with nine other beauties, she was being garlanded, robed in a gown made of cloth from the tapa tree, and perfumed in readiness for a ceremony—the launching of a new canoe.

She was delighted to see him, and with signs and gestures introduced him to her mother, her aunt, and her sisters, who were attending to her.

When it was time for the ceremony Casca went with them to the beach.

Once again the whole village seemed to be present. The canoe was a splendid vessel, dug out of a forest giant from high on the mountain. Many months, the greater part of a year, had been needed to sled the canoe down the mountainside, the craftsmen hollowing it as they moved it day by day. At last, completed and elaborately carved, they had hauled it to the beach.

A glance told Casca that the huge vessel could not possibly be moved by the few men who could get a handhold on it, nor could it be sledded across the soft sand to the water, and rollers of logs would merely be pushed into the sand by the canoe's great weight. He was interested to see just how this launching was to be accomplished.

Twenty husky warriors took up positions on either side of the great canoe. Each of them seized one of the carved handholds along the gunwale. The wooden drums started up, the warriors chanted, and on the fifth beat a great shout came from every throat in the village. The twenty men heaved with all their might.

And the canoe moved a few inches.

Casca looked down the broad expanse of beach and quickly calculated that the effort needed to get the canoe to the water would exhaust not only these twenty warriors, but the entire village. As far as he could see, this method simply wouldn't work.

Alesia danced lightly forward to a different rhythm from the drums. She was a vision of delight, her beautiful little bosom vibrating in time to the beat.

The drums stopped, then started again. Once more the warriors grasped the canoe.

A horrible idea came into Casca's mind as Alesia gracefully sank to the ground, to lie on the sand in front of the prow of the canoe.

Of a sudden Casca knew that his horrible idea was right. The chant had reached the fourth beat. Casca leaped to his feet.

An enormous shout erupted from every throat. Casca found himself screaming, too, and the twenty warriors heaved.

Alesia's hips and her lovely legs twirled in a macabre dance in the air as the canoe's great length rolled over her, the elaborate robes of tapa cloth torn away.

Now her feet pointed together to the sky and her pelvis struck the sand, her luscious buttocks vibrating as if in orgasm. Now she lay again on her back, legs spread wide apart so that despite his horror, Casca's eyes were glued to the small, black bush where the legs met.

The legs writhed and kicked, the knees opened and closed in spasms. Then the canoe was turning her onto her belly once more as the warriors shouted and heaved.

The beautiful legs kicked skyward as her back broke, then crashed limply to the sand. The canoe moved faster,

the now blood-drenched legs flailed about limply as the
body was turned over and over, the pushing warriors dancing nimbly to avoid them.

Then the stern of the canoe was clear of her body, the
men still pushing, the canoe sliding farther, greased with
the girl's body fats, the sand firmed with her blood.

The canoe stopped and the exhausted warriors fell to the
sand alongside it, their chests heaving, mouths sagging
open as they gasped for air.

A great groan escaped from Casca.

From all sides there came the same sound.

Then everybody was moving slowly toward where the
body lay, almost severed in two parts. Though he couldn't
tell why, Casca was moving with the others. He didn't
want to look at the body, yet felt impelled toward it.

First to reach the mangled corpse were some old women
carrying calabashes of water and tapa cloths. In a few moments they had washed the body clean and redressed Alesia
as she had been just a few minutes earlier.

With a long, sad sigh Casca lowered himself to the
sand. All the villagers squatted on the sand too. They sat
and the drums started up again. The people clapped slowly
and everybody sang.

Casca found himself singing too. He had no idea of the
words nor their meaning. The bodies of the singers swayed
as if in time to the paddle strokes of a great canoe carrying
a loved one to some far off pleasant place. The song went
on but would be interrupted nine more times by the continuing sacrifices.

When the second girl stood ready for the ceremony it
had occurred to Casca to intervene. But the man of action
was stayed by his own considerable confusion.

By now the Roman had known some tens of thousands
of women, and killed perhaps that many men and not a few
women by his own hands, and ten or maybe a hundred
times that many by his orders.

So why such concern?

He had hardly known Alesia. Her cousin, who was now
dancing before the prow of the canoe, he didn't know at

all. But his mind revolted at such a waste of beauty. Of lovely, desirable, usable women.

In his loins Casca felt the stirrings of a vague, undefinable desire. Another emotion was replacing the horror. Now he wanted to see the girl lie down, and as he recognized the thought she did so. The warriors seized the canoe. The chant quickly reached its climax.

And Casca was on his feet with everybody else, screaming.

Again the tapa robes were torn apart. This girl had lain with her head toward Casca, and the sight was truly horrible as her eyes bulged, her tongue protruded, her arms shot out, the fingers extended with tremendous energy. Her bosom heaved and the nipples sprouted erect.

As the moving canoe turned her onto her belly her back arched, her arms above her head as if she would rise from under the boat's great weight.

Then it rolled her once more onto her back and she did rise, almost as if to clutch the gunwale of the boat with her hands. A torrent of blood vomited from her mouth.

The canoe moved on relentlessly, and once more she was on her belly, her beautiful body arched backward, her breasts pointing with fierce energy at Casca, her upraised arms reaching for the sky.

The canoe turned her over again, her back broke and she flopped to the sand. The canoe slid on and on, and she rolled with it, lifeless now, her arms turning loosely, the hands softly patting at the sand.

Then it was over and Casca was on his feet, moving once more toward the body with everybody else. And a few minutes later he was sitting with the others, clapping slowly and singing, the girl lying at peace, washed clean and redressed in fresh robes, as if she'd died comfortably.

What monstrousness, Casca was thinking once again. But he also saw that the canoe was closer to the water, and he searched his experience for some other way to accomplish this.

Clearly log rollers would not work. The weight of the canoe would simply bury the first log in the sand. The sand could, perhaps, be firmed with water from the sea, but how to carry so much water so far and quickly enough? And how to keep the sand wet in the broiling heat?

He abandoned this thinking. With the sacrifice of each new girl he grew more and more carnally excited; excited, too, to see the canoe getting closer and closer to the sea. Now he was cheering on the pushers; applauding in his mind the twirling of the girl's body; waiting, when her feet were toward him, for that moment when her legs would shoot wide apart; desire surging through him as the young cunt stretched open, and then again, when she was turned over and her ass pounded her pussy into the sand like a frantic young girl riding a lover to her own orgasm.

And as the back broke he felt something very much like orgasm, and his raging, conflicting emotions of horror, excitement, pity, and desire, were replaced by feelings of sympathy, affection, and gratitude.

He was grateful, and knew that all around him this was the climactic emotion of all the people. Sacrifice by sacrifice the great canoe was getting closer to the sea, moving toward the end of its year-long passage from the mountaintop where the tree had grown to maturity.

For many more years now, for countless years, this canoe would serve the village, provide it with fish and turtles and the beautiful things that came from the sea— corals, and great, lovely shells, and sometimes pearls.

And in war this canoe would carry its warriors into battle to protect the village, or to attack another village and carry home the spoils.

By the end of the day, at the cost of ten beautiful women, the canoe was in the water. Seeing people killed was no new experience for Casca, and he'd seen women killed much more horribly. He had even seen women he loved die horrible deaths, tortured, torn apart, chopped to pieces, eaten by wild animals. But for some reason that he couldn't explain to himself, this day had affected him more powerfully.

Perhaps, he reasoned, it was the calm way each successive girl took her place in front of the canoe as her turn came. And the placid acceptance of her mangled corpse by her relatives. The whole ceremony impressed Casca as disgustingly barbarous, and yet there was something highly civilized about it.

If Casca was badly affected by the launching, the rest of the company of the *Rangaroa* were all but destroyed. Young Sandy had fainted when the canoe first rolled over Alesia. Liam had become hysterical when he saw his lover of the previous night about to take her turn before the bloodstained prow. Larsen had been reduced to a sobbing heap of unhappiness. Ulf simply sat in the sand, occasionally opening his eyes to see a few moments of one or the other of the grisly deaths, then shaking his head, gritting his teeth and closing his eyes again.

The bodies of the ten girls were laid in the great canoe, each one's head resting in another's lap. The twenty warriors waded alongside the canoe, then swam with it, pushing it toward the opening in the reef and through it out into the open sea.

The sun was just setting, and in the fading light Casca could just see them overturn the boat, then push it back inside the lagoon.

"Damn fools," he muttered to Ulf, "why the fuck don't they get into the boat? Right on sunset there'll be sharks aplenty out there after those bodies."

Ulf shrugged. He had quite recovered his normal cold cynicism. "In these parts you got to take your fun as you find it. You got to admit it keeps life interesting."

Casca snorted the contempt of the professional for thrill seekers. "Just bloody stupid. They're not even hurrying— coming back slower than they went out. Nothing on earth would get me—or you—out there with those idiots."

"Me, no," Ulf grunted, "you, if you stay here a year you'll be competing for a place in the team."

"The hell I will," Casca snapped, wondering at his concern as he realized that he was straining into the growing darkness with every fiber of his being, as if he could drag the twenty men to safety.

At last, still upside down, the great canoe slid onto the

beach and the warriors lay beside it, recovering their breath.

Casca let out his own breath in a great long sigh which was echoed all around him. A drum beat and a new chant commenced, and Casca realized that this was the first sound since the bodies had left the beach two hours earlier.

In the song Casca repeatedly heard Alesia's name, and guessed that he was hearing a new song that might be sung for years into the future—certainly for the life of the canoe. The song named each girl over and over, describing her and telling the story of her life and of her part in the launching of the canoe.

The song went on all night. At sunrise everybody walked into the lagoon and washed in the salt water, then turned and walked back to the village, talking quietly as they went.

The *Rangaroa* crew did the same, but lingered on the beach together, a little dismayed and overwhelmed by the day's events, and wondering what might come next. After a while they, too, walked up the hill into the village.

For the villagers another ordinary day was already in full swing. Women were cooking, men working, children playing.

"Dis bit I understand," said Ulf. "In Greenland when we launch a new boat, everybody get drunk. Next day just work like normal."

CHAPTER EIGHT

The next day Casca felt better. He walked through the village and discovered that for the villagers it was as if the ceremony had never happened. He visited Alesia's house. Her mother and her aunt were chatting as they made tapa cloth, laughing as if she had never existed.

The bark had been carefully stripped from the tree in sheets, soaked in water and pounded between stones to produce a fabric as soft as silk on the skin and as cool as cotton in the heat of the tropic sun. Now the women were using a sort of woodblock to decorate the fabric with elaborate designs that told meaningful stories, recounted legends, or set symbolic examples.

That night, as far as Casca could tell, the conversation in the chief's house was entirely about other matters. It was as if the people only had a memory span of a few hours.

Or perhaps it was simply that the disturbing news that had reached the island from the nearby Fiji isles put all other matters out of mind.

Cakabau, the chief of the tiny island of Bau, had declared himself king of all of Fiji and the islands to the west, which included Navola Levu. Kini came from a village that had been subjugated by this bloodthirsty and power-hungry chief, and the elders of the village were interested

53

to hear whatever he could tell them. They sat with Kini, Casca, and several members of the *Rangaroa* crew while the *bilo*—the coconut kava cup—was passed back and forth.

The old chief nodded knowingly. "Here in our mountain fastness we are invincible. It is impossible for an enemy to kill one of our men before we kill one of his, so long as we choose to stay behind our palisade."

"Which we don't very often do," Mbolo said. It seemed to Casca that Mbolo, educated in English by the wandering merchant adventurer Samuel Clevinger, was almost as important as Semele.

Sonolo, a massively built young man, shrugged and spread wide his enormous hands. "Well, after all, that is the way we are. Naturally we prefer to go out and greet the enemy and fight him where there is more danger."

Semele paused, pursed his lips in thought for a moment, then spoke: "But is it not clear that against Cakabau we cannot afford to be so adventurous? Should we meet him outside the palisade and he kill one of our men, we would pay a great price for our adventurousness, Sonolo."

It seemed to Casca that he must be missing or misunderstanding something of this conversation.

"Excuse me," he said, "but I don't quite understand. Do you mean to say that the fighting stops as soon as one man is killed?"

He looked into a number of uncomprehending faces.

Sonolo, who was the war chief and a nephew of Semele, answered him. "But of course. Surely one dead man is enough."

"Well," Casca shrugged, "from the point of view of the one, I guess it's one too many. But what if you should lose a man when you have the advantage?"

Semele looked at Casca as if he suddenly had doubts of his intellect.

"What advantage could offset the death of a man?"

Casca shrugged and sat staring up at the thatch roof, looking for an answer from his long experience of civilized warfare that would make sense to these man-eating barbarians who could not conceive of a war that would kill more than one man.

"But Cakabau, too, is invincible," Kini told the chief.

"Perhaps he is, on his island of Bau, but we do not think of attacking Bau."

"That is not what I mean," said Kini. "He is invincible wherever he goes."

"How can this be?" asked Semele, puzzled.

"He carries with him six weapons of enormous power."

Semele laughed. "I will be very happy to meet Cakabau in battle if he is silly enough to carry six clubs. No man could wield even two clubs effectively."

"These weapons are not clubs, and Cakabau himself only carries one of them, but they can kill a man from a distance of ten tens of paces."

The old chief looked intently into Kini's eyes. "You have seen these weapons?"

"I have seen them. On our island of Vanua Levu we met Cakabau and his raiders on the beach and three of our men were killed from a great distance."

"Hmm." Semele scratched his grizzled head. "Hmm. We have heard of these fire-stick weapons, but we thought the tales exaggerated. This is something new which must be taken into consideration."

Ateca, a tiny woman who seemed to be the chief's number one wife, spoke: "Can the stones that these fire sticks throw pierce our palisade?"

"Not readily, I think," Kini replied.

"Then here we remain invincible," said Semele, "but outside our palisade we are vulnerable." He turned again to Kini. "What is Cakabau's vulnerability?"

Kini shook his head. "Alas, none has found it."

Semele looked grim. "Then it is clear. We must acquire this form of invincibility or we are doomed. From whence came his weapons?"

"From the Valangi," Kini replied.

"Valangi—the whites," Sandy whispered to Casca. "Makes you feel proud, eh?"

"And why did the Valangi give him weapons?"

"He gave them men for the weapons," Kini glowered. "Our men."

"Mmm." Semele slowly moved his great head in circles, first one way with an expression like that of a puzzled child, then the other way with increasing realization. "So, they gave him the weapons before he gave them the men?"

"Of course," Kini spat. "The men of Bau would not try to take our men without these weapons."

Again Semele rotated his head in the puzzled manner. "Are not the Valangi afraid that the Tui Bau will turn the guns on them, take their men and eat them?"

Kini laughed, but bitterly. "The Valangi are not afraid, because they have bigger weapons—as big to these weapons as you are to a baby."

Semele stopped moving his head. His face was all consternation as he gasped: "How can this be? Who could carry such a weapon?"

"They carry them on their great canoes, such as the one I came here on. They make a great fire on the ship and then there is a terrible noise on the ship, and then the noise and the fire and many large stones are in the village, and many dead people are everywhere. I do not know how."

Semele looked at Larsen. "Do you have such weapons on your great canoe?"

"I do not," Larsen said. "We have no weapons aboard." He had decided early in this conversation to say nothing of his ship's small brass cannon, nor of the muskets and a revolver concealed in his cabin.

Casca was relieved at his reply, although he guessed there would be some arms concealed aboard somewhere, just as he had his small .38 in his jacket pocket. He patted it lightly.

The old chief asked more and more questions, and Kini looked unhappy as they extended more and more into areas he didn't understand. Yet he wanted to provide the much needed information.

"There is much of this business of the Valangi that I do not understand, Semele. None can understand."

"Then tell us without understanding," said Semele. "Perhaps our Valangi friends here can explain."

Kini spread his hands wide in a gesture of incomprehension. "Amongst the Valangi there is only one God, the one called Jesus. But they have many different . . . many different . . ." He gave up. It was beyond understanding.

"Different what?" Semele pressed.

"I hardly know, chief. Different men—they are called preachers—who talk to this Jesus in different ways. But these different preachers—some agree, others differ."

"According to their villages," Ateca said.

Kini looked bewildered. "No, that is what none can understand. The ones who agree come from many different villages, from many different islands, different countries, different flags, yet they agree. Others from the same country, same village, like London or Boston or Sydney, they do not agree. And these different preachers encourage their believers to attack each other—not for land, or for food, or for women—but so as to convert the others to their own way of talking to this Jesus."

"I don't understand," said Semele.

"It is not to be understood," said Kini.

Semele looked inquiringly at Larsen and Casca and Sandy.

They all shrugged. "Truly," said Larsen, "it is not to be understood."

"But how is this disagreement to do with the weapons?" Ateca asked.

"Aha, yes, what of the weapons?" asked Semele.

"The weapons come from a Captain Savage, a trader and missionary Valangi, who wishes to convert everybody to his method of talking to Jesus. He calls it Methodist."

"What does he trade in, this Savage?"

"Men, Semele, he deals only in men."

For a long time Semele sat looking at the floor. Then for a long time he stared at the roof. At last he spoke. "Will this Savage sell us guns if we give him men?"

Kini's eyes started from his head. "If you . . . I do not

know. I do not know. I do not like to think about such a thing."

"And I do not like to think about it," said Semele, "but now it is necessary to do some thinking."

"But this is evil thinking."

"Of course it is. But if what we hear from Viti Levu is true, and I fear it is, Cakabau has already done this thinking. We are told that he has already offered for sale all the men of our village, and that he has already been paid much money. Now he must take our men. And what is a village without men? It is the end of the world for us."

CHAPTER NINE

The next morning Casca awoke beside Vivita, a slim, quiet woman who had—he couldn't tell how—won him from three or four competing women the previous night. But he was glad she had won.

She was not beautiful. Her forehead was too high, her nose too broad, the nostrils large and flared, her lips thick, a front tooth missing. But her slim body was a fount of sexual energy, and her placid silences were pleasant to be around.

She gestured to him that he should get up quickly, that there was much happening. She pointed toward the beach and toward the chief's house, and made gestures of fighting.

She brought him a length of tapa cloth and showed him how to wrap himself in it, forming a *sulu*, the long kilt worn by men throughout the South Pacific.

"*Vanaka vaka levu*, thank you very much," Casca said, appreciating the admiration in Vivita's eyes now that he was dressed like any other warrior. But how to carry his gun and knife?

He put on his jacket, and Vivita clapped her hands in delight. Reassured, he added his belt, but left his arms concealed in his jacket pockets.

Casca hurried to the chief's house, on the way noting

that there were many strange canoes drawn up on the beach
and many strange warriors standing around them.

From Semele he learned that these men came from Lakuvi, a village on the other side of the island, a traditional
enemy. The lands that the people of Lakuvi farmed ran up
toward the village of Navola, and they laid claim to some
of the coconut trees and breadfruit trees that belonged to
Navola. The dispute had been going on forever, every so
often leading to wars between the two villages.

The battles resolved nothing about the long-standing
dispute but were welcomed by both sides, since each battle
meant that one village or the other was likely to feast on
meat that night.

If the men from Lakuvi won the battle, the killed Navola man would be partly eaten on the beach in front of the
village and the remains taken back to Lakuvi for a feast in
their own village. The victors would also strip Navola's
fruit trees and taro patches of their food, and the disputed
trees on the far slopes of the mountain would for a time
belong to Lakuvi.

If Navola won, as the defending village usually did, the
slain man would be eaten, the trees would become their
undisputed property for a while, and they would also seize
most of the enemy's weapons and some of their canoes.

But just now, as far as Casca could see, the battle was
going in a very leisurely manner. The men below on the
beach were making no preparations for attack, and the Navola villagers appeared quite unconcerned, going about
their normal tasks, working in their food gardens, cooking,
children playing about.

Eventually the men below on the beach began beating
drums and forming up in something like battle order—
drawn up in three ranks, chanting, shouting and waving
their great, black war clubs.

Casca spoke to Semele and was given a beautiful, shiny
club, about the heaviest weapon he had ever hefted. It was
the root of a tree that grew deep in remote jungle, the root
branches cut short to sharp knobs. The wood was ex-
tremely hard, heavy, and very unlikely to split or break

even when pounded against another similar club. When pounded with all the force of a warrior's arm against a man's head, death was the inevitable result.

After some long time the enemy moved up the hill toward the village and a number of Navola warriors formed up and began to dance and chant too.

The enemy moved farther up the hill, stopped again, danced and chanted, and the men of Navola replied.

When the Lakuvi warriors appeared at the top of the rise the Navola men moved outside the outermost of the three palisades and the two groups danced, chanted, and threatened each other.

The Lakuvi men moved closer. The Navola men moved farther from the palisade to confront them.

For some hours the two squads maneuvered about the open flat space outside the palisade, each seeking an opening that would make an attack worthwhile.

Casca grew tired of watching the ceremonious maneuvering from his perch with the *Rangaroa* crew on the top rail of the outer palisade. Semele had confided to him his fear that the attack might have been planned in cooperation with Cakabau to test Navola's defenses, and prepare the way for a full-scale attack with the Bau chief's fearsome weapons.

Casca turned from the maneuvers. The battle would not be joined unless one side felt sure of an advantage and of their skills. Forces and arms were so evenly matched that this might take a very long time.

"Well enough," Casca said to himself, "but what if Cakabau should arrive with his muskets?"

Navola's troops were led by Sonolo, and Casca admired the way his club-wielding warriors danced forward and back, maneuvered from one side of the small plateau to the other and back in aggressive feints or in response to threats from the Lakuvi warriors.

But if Cakabau's men were to arrive, all Sonolo's brilliance would be irrelevant with the first shots. And Cakabau's men did not just kill one man. Their six muskets usually killed six men, and notoriously they might then go

on a rampage, killing and eating great numbers of the
enemy. The musket had radically changed the practice of
war in the islands.

Casca tried to think of how the crucified one's curse
would keep him alive or bring him back to life if he were
chewed up and digested in a dozen different cannibal's
stomachs.

Would he live on in some other form? Many different
forms according to where the cannibal's bodies excreted
his pieces? A number of soldier ants perhaps, with some
sort of group consciousness that used to be Casca Rufio
Longinus? He knew something very like terror as he
thought about it. Nor did he relish the alternative prospect
of underfed and overworked slavery on the Australian
sugar plantations.

He turned and ran . . . across the open space to the second palisade, where the lounging defenders glanced at him
curiously . . . across the next open space to the inner palisade, and across the next space . . . past the chief's house,
across the village square, past the houses and toward the
inner rear palisade.

He cleared the six-foot fence in his stride, the two horizontal rails and the outward-leaning slope of the fence as-
sisting him, as they were designed to do.

He cleared the next two palisades similarly, ignoring the
surprised looks of the few warriors posted at the rear to
guard against a sneak attack from this direction.

He raced down the eastern slope of the hill until he was
sure he was lower than the attackers on the western slope,
then turned and raced back around the northern slope to
come up behind and below the enemy warriors.

He crept up the slope until he was within pistol shot of
the three ranks of warriors with their backs to him.

He put down his club and took the five-shot .38 from
his jacket pocket, checked the load, and stuck it in his belt.

"If I have to use you to win this, I'm just no damned
good," he muttered.

He looked along the line of broad, black backs, each

with a huge, black club, and he patted the spare ammunition in his pocket.

"But if it comes to it, I'd sure rather be no damned good than chopped up."

He shook his head in astonishment. He hadn't felt like this in a long time, maybe a couple of centuries.

"What the fuck is happening to me? Am I falling in love with life?" He recalled his bout of seasickness when the curse of an eternity of soldiering looked positively inviting compared to one more minute of seasickness, and any form of death more inviting still.

He picked up the great war club and raced up the rest of the slope, heading for the last man in the rear rank. A few yards short, the man heard or sensed him and half turned. Casca let out a great whoop and hurled himself forward, the great club swinging for the thick helmet of black hair.

The blow never reached home. Taken by surprise as he was, the Lakuvi warrior just had time to bring up his club and block the blow.

The shock of the impact very nearly wrenched the club from Casca's grasp. The warrior was knocked out of the line and a little away from his comrades.

Sonolo couldn't see Casca and didn't know what was happening, but realized there was some disturbance in that corner of the enemy's ranks and feinted for the other side.

The Lakuvi squad danced away, leaving Casca and the single warrior on their own.

The warrior hurled himself at Casca. He managed to block the blow, but again almost lost the club.

"Shit, this isn't as easy as it looks," he muttered as he aimed another flailing blow at the black head.

Again the muscle-wrenching clash, and Casca felt his arm growing numb. And the nearest of the enemy warriors was now turning in his direction, their front ranks having succeeded in parrying Sonolo's blind feint.

Casca wearily brought up the club as his enemy swung for his head. At the last moment, instead of parrying the blow with his club, he pivoted on his heel, swaying out of the way. The momentum of his effort carried the warrior past him, and Casca continued his pivot and brought a crashing blow down on the back of his head.

Too late, he thought, as he saw three more enemy rushing toward him. He dropped the club and pulled the revolver from his belt.

But the enemy warriors stopped dead as they saw their comrade fall. They dropped their clubs and turned and ran away down the slope. In another second the rest of the Lakuvi men realized what had happened and ran too. The war chief, last to see the defeat, turned and ran after them.

Now Sonolo realized what had happened and came running to Casca, whooping delightedly as he hugged him. In a second he was surrounded by gleeful warriors all trying to hug him.

They picked up the unconscious enemy and lifted him above their heads. From the palisade came a great cheer, then a louder one as everybody inside the village realized that they were victorious.

Half a dozen warriors carried the body to the village while the others raced after the retreating enemy to secure some of their canoes. Abandoned clubs were all over the field. Casca accompanied the body into the village, surrounded by the entire population cheering lustily.

Casca noticed that the body was carried with respect, almost with affection. As it was placed on the ground in the square he saw that some of the women who had been cheering so lustily only a moment earlier were now crying.

A number of men were digging a hole and others were bringing stones and firewood and pots full of hot coals. Women were bringing great armfuls of banana leaves and calabashes and gourds full of water.

Semele squatted cross-legged on the ground, and the unconscious warrior was placed before him, the feet toward him. Those who had carried the body ended their slow chant and also squatted beside the body. Casca stood looking down at the man's head. He seemed to be in a deep coma, and would no doubt be dead very soon.

Semele beckoned Casca, and when he approached the old chief stood up, indicating that Casca should sit in his place. Casca did so and a great cheer went up from all the village people.

Sandy had appeared from somewhere. "He's just made you a chief, mon," he said. "You're a war chief now, I'm thinkin'."

Casca realized that Sandy was right.

"Hell," he muttered, "I don't want the job."

"Don't say it too loud or you'll be stuck with it for life. They distrust ambition and only reward performance."

Casca shrugged. Well, why the hell not? He'd led armies often enough before. This wouldn't be so different.

Ateca came toward the dying warrior, carrying a green-stone axe, the sun glinting from the razor-sharp blade. She stood between Casca and the enemy, chanting slowly. She held the head of the axe toward Casca, then turned gracefully, raising it high above her head.

Casca felt his own testicles leap up into his pelvic cavity as the axe was buried in the ground with a dull thump, severing the warrior's genitals from his body.

A great cheer went up.

Ateca picked up the severed piece and inserted a green twig into the root of the penis. As the stick stretched the penis to about erect length there were shrieks and giggles from the women and laughs and grunts from the men.

The fire in the pit was now roaring, and Ateca held the meat out over the fringe of the fire, carefully toasting it, continually withdrawing it before it burned.

Casca was so intrigued by this South Pacific cuisine that for a moment he failed to notice what was happening to the rest of the body. Two women were squatting between the still breathing man's legs, reaching into the body cavity through the hole that Ateca had opened and dragging out handfuls of intestines which they passed to a number of small children, who ran around dragging the entrails about like lengths of rope. Other women were spearing the heart, lungs, liver, and kidneys on twigs and holding them out over the edge of the flames.

Ateca placed the cooked meat on a banana leaf and presented it to Casca.

He stared, horror stricken, at the penis, the outer skin crisped to black-brown and split apart by the heat, showing the pink lightly cooked meat inside. The testicles had shrunk to the size of grapes.

Repressing a shudder, Casca looked around. The other organs were being shared out among the village elders. The heart was on a banana leaf before Semele, and the old chief sat waiting, looking expectantly at Casca.

"You're holding up dinner, your chiefness," he heard Sandy say as he realized that he was expected to start the feast.

He couldn't possibly do it. Then he looked up at the hundred expectant faces and realized that he couldn't possibly not do it.

"Oh, no," he groaned.

"Sweetbreads we call 'em at home." Sandy chuckled. "They're considered a delicacy. 'Course, we get 'em off bulls." He chuckled some more and all the people around joined in.

The fire pit was now being filled with stones, and women were hacking the body into pieces, wrapping each piece in banana leaves and placing them on the hot stones together with enormous quantities of taro, cassava, and yams. Then the pit was filled in, covering the meat with earth.

He heard a sharp intake of breath and glanced around to see that the smile had left Sandy's face as he was handed the man's barbecued liver. "Oy mon, I don't think I can do this," he groaned.

A polite cough from the old chief alerted Casca that he had stalled about as long as politeness would allow. All around him men were waiting for him to eat so that they, too, could start on the tasty morsels before them.

"They call roasted man long pig," Larsen said. "It's probably not so bad."

"An acquired taste I suppose," Casca muttered, and picking up the prick, chewed off one of the balls.

To his amazement he found the meat tender and tasty.

He looked around him at the grinning faces as a dozen men followed his example and began to eat. Semele took to the heart with gusto, but the others took one big bite of their piece of offal and passed the rest along.

Relieved to discover this way out of his predicament, Casca, while chewing lustily on one of the late departed's most precious possessions, passed the rest to the man next to him.

The reaction was immediate, and on all sides Casca saw consternation. Everybody had stopped eating and they were looking worriedly at Casca. He didn't need to be told that he was about to create a bad omen. If the war chief did not wish to eat the vanquished foe, it would clearly suggest doubt about the victory.

He moved quickly to dispel any such notions.

He stood, belched, farted, thumped his chest and sat again on the floor, taking back the banana leaf and quickly biting off the other testicle.

The cannibals shrugged and returned their attention to their meal. They didn't understand Casca's little routine, and probably presumed that it was a custom amongst whites when they were eating their enemies. They returned their attention to what they were eating while Casca tried to decide which end of the penis would be the least revolting to start chewing. A disinclination to take the head into his mouth made him decide to start at the base, and he found the meat even tastier than the pig organ he had eaten two months earlier in San Francisco.

The children had now tired of their rope game and were racing for the sea, whooping and shouting and dragging with them the many yards of the warrior's entrails, the contents of which were smeared all over their bodies.

They leaped laughing into the water and sat in the shallows, inch by inch squeezing out the excreta from the intestines and thoroughly washing them in the sea.

When the fire pit was opened and the leaf-wrapped parcels of meat were passed around, Casca was in turn presented with an arm and a leg, but to his immense relief he

was only expected to nibble a mouthful and pass along the
rest. He then made a great show of eating a great deal,
keeping his mouth and his hands full of the vegetable roots
so that nobody thought to offer him more meat.

In a remarkably short space of time there was nothing
left of the enemy but a few bones that children were breaking open with stones to get at the marrow. The whole village had participated in the feast, so that nobody had eaten
more than a few mouthfuls of the body.

Yet the meat seemed to have a strange effect. Some of
the younger warriors who may have eaten more than anybody else were staggering about as though drunk. Several
of them were crudely fondling girls who were responding
lewdly and enthusiastically, although until now Casca had
seen only the most modest behavior in public. He felt himself to be on the edge of stupor and had to struggle to stay
awake, while all around him there developed something
like one of the orgies he once used to attend in Rome.

Some music started up on the wooden drums and the
stringed instruments, and men and women began to dance.
Their movements and gestures became increasingly sen-
sual, the dancers getting more and more excited.

From time to time a couple would stop dancing, seize
each other hungrily and quickly leave the scene, almost
running into the jungle or behind a house, anywhere, it
seemed, where they could quickly set about satisfying their
raging lust. Some of them barely bothered to get out of
sight.

Others would leave the dancing and come to where most
of the people were seated and dance before them, offering
themselves to the one they had chosen.

A number of pretty young girls did this before Casca,
and two or three times he was about to get to his feet and
accept their offer when suddenly the girl would turn and go
back to the other dancers.

When this happened yet again Casca saw the moment
when the girl changed her mind. She looked as if she'd
been threatened.

Casca looked behind him to see the seated Vivita looking up at the girl. The expression on her face was more of disdain than anger, her mouth partly open, drawn down at the corners, her eyes staring coldly at the younger girl.

The girl seemed to be in heat, and for a little while tried to ignore Vivita's cold stare, concentrating on displaying her charms to Casca. He was fascinated at the duel between the two women, and lusting for the younger one, who was surely his for the taking. He watched Vivita carefully, but she didn't glance at him.

The hell with it, he decided. After all, I am a war chief, the hero of the day, and I'm being offered one of the fruits of victory. If I had to chew my way through that damned cooked prick, I might as well accept what's being offered here too.

He started to rise, glancing at Vivita, who still ignored him but jerked her head up to concentrate her gaze on the eyes of the lewdly dancing girl. The girl's eyes fell, the fire went out of her dance, and she backed away.

Annoyed, Casca turned to look at Vivita. Now she returned his look with a slight smile and a meaningful tilt of her head toward the hut where they had slept. Strong desire for this powerful woman seized Casca, and he got to his feet. Vivita's smile broadened and Casca found himself enchanted by her gap-toothed grin as she, too, got up. With his arm around her they headed for the hut.

Vivita's slow, calm demeanor concealed the urges within her that had been fired by the rare treat of red meat. She hungrily twined her body to Casca's and sank with him to the grass sleeping mat, her hands and lips and breasts and thighs all trying to join with him at once in a frenzy of desire that grew and grew and did not diminish when she quickly reached an orgasm.

Her urgent demands didn't cease as Casca strove to please her, wondering where he himself found the sustained energy. Vivita pushed her body against his, her arms and legs enwrapping him completely, her mouth devouring his. Only when Casca at last collapsed in a long-delayed shuddering climax did she relax, but still held him to her.

In what seemed only a few minutes she renewed her demands. Casca responded willingly enough, but wondered whether he would be able to match her seemingly unlimited desires. The thought crossed his mind that it was a damn good thing that wars amongst these cannibals ended with the eating of only one man.

CHAPTER TEN

The next morning just before sunrise Vivita served him a breakfast of fish soup and cassava, and again alerted him that this was a day of much activity in the village and that he should be out and about and participating.

He made his way to the chief's house, meeting along the way Sandy and Ulf, who had been similarly sent from their huts by their women. Most of the men of the village seemed to be present, and shortly Larsen and others of the *Rangaroa*'s crew arrived.

Everybody seemed very much at ease, and there was none of the tension or excitement of the previous morning. Casca could not quite tell what was going on, but it was clear he was not important in it. Looking around, he noticed Sonolo and saw that he, too, seemed to have been relegated to a position of unimportance.

Semele and Mbolo were conferring mainly with Sakuvi, whom Casca had seen previously in positions of honor but had not heard participating in this fashion. Today, however, Sakuvi seemed to be in charge.

And so it proved. At a word from Sukuvi everybody moved off, as if to some long-standing arrangement, and Casca noticed that several of the men carried bulging tapa sacks. The crew of the *Rangaroa* tagged on to the end of the party as they left the village and walked for about a

mile, climbing the slopes of the mountain until they came
to a small plateau.

Casca was faintly puzzled. If he had correctly understood what he'd heard about the terrain, they must be getting close to the territory disputed with the Lakuvi village.

They stopped at a large, cleared patch of ground which
looked as if it had been prepared for sowing with some sort
of crop. Digging sticks, axes, and other implements lay
about the field.

Casca was pleased to see all these tools, as he had noticed that none of the men carried any sort of weapon, so
that should the Lakuvi attack them, his .38 would have
been the only defense available. He didn't doubt that it
would be sufficient, unless Cakabau's muskets should also
arrive.

Men picked up the implements and studied them as if
they had never seen them before, comparing one with another and making complimentary or disparaging remarks
about them.

As usual the bright young Scot was the first of the white
men to understand what was going on. "Oy, mon, it's
planting time. It's farmers we're going to be today. I'll bet
this is the land that's been won from the enemy."

Men were opening the sacks, upending them to tip out
carefully cut pieces of taro, cassava, and sweet potato.
Within a few minutes everybody was at work, digging
holes, planting seeds, and covering them with earth. Casca
and the crew joined in somewhat awkwardly, neither soldiering nor sailing being ideal preparation for farming. But
they were soon working diligently along with the others.

The sun climbed the sky and the day grew hotter and
hotter, but the work showed no sign of slackening. Casca
enjoyed it, sweat running from every pore of his body.

When the sun was high in the sky a number of women
appeared, carrying on their heads great pots of water and
parcels wrapped in banana leaves. They placed these on the
ground and squatted beside them.

The men continued working their way along the planting rows until they came close to the women. Then they

would stop and squat alongside them. Casca and the crew followed suit, and when everybody was sitting, the women opened the packages and distributed the food—whole small fish, breadfruit, cassava and taro, papayas and bananas.

Vivita was among the women, but she paid no attention to Casca, and chatted only with the other women. Although there was some conversation between the men and the women, it was collective and quite impersonal.

Casca ate hungrily, washing down the food with some of the water. He noticed that there was a great deal of water, and more women arrived carrying yet more, which they placed around the edges of the field.

As the men finished eating they went back to work and the women headed off down the hill to the village.

Casca worked contentedly for some hours. He was just beginning to think that he'd had about enough farming for one day when he noticed that men were stopping work as they came to the end of a row, congregating at one end of the field. He quickly finished the row he was working on and joined them.

Conversation was brisk and lighthearted. Casca could barely understand any of it, but it seemed to be concerned with the day's work and general farming matters.

As the sun dipped behind the mountain and threw cool shade over the field, the men got up from their rest and took up the pots that the women had placed around the field, using them to water the new plantings. Then everybody headed off down the mountain toward the village.

Along the way they crossed a small stream and dipped the pots full of clear mountain water. Then they bathed away the sweat and the dirt of the day's work, the grown men gamboling in the water like little boys.

Heading back to the village, they carried the water with them, and Casca noticed that it took two men carrying the pots between them by the handles to carry down the mountain what each woman had carried up on her head.

When they arrived back at the village the evening meal

was cooking, several women busy inside the cooking house. Many more were sitting around outside, chatting.

Each little group of women sat around an earthenware pot, and from time to time one or another of them would lean over the pot and spit what was in her mouth into it. Then she would take another mouthful of a stringy looking root and go back to chewing.

Casca was intrigued. No men, not even the smallest boys, were chewing upon the root, and Casca had never seen this root presented at a meal.

"What is this root?" he asked.

Setole, Mbolo's sister, who was almost as big as her brother, smiled up at him as she leaned forward to dribble a mouthful into the pot.

"Kava," she said. "We make it now, you drink tonight."

Casca managed to nod and smile as he moved away from the unedifying scene as quickly as he could.

"So that's why the women don't drink it at night," Liam laughed, "they've already had the best of it."

For the next several days Casca spent his time with the farmers, enjoying the work, the cheerful company, the after-work bath in the stream, and then the huge nightly meal and the long, relaxing kava session in the chief's house.

From these nights in the chief's house Casca got an insight into the everyday management of the village. With neither the threat of war nor the excitement of the special event of the arrival of the *Rangaroa,* he saw that there was a considerable change in people's roles.

The young women no longer occupied the front of the room, as they had on the night that the *Rangaroa* arrived, but chatted quietly at the back while the older women, wives, and mothers took a very lively part in every discussion.

Semele and Mbolo still occupied the most privileged positions, but where on earlier nights had sat the war chiefs, Sonolo and Casca, and the principal warriors, these places were now occupied by Sakuvi and Dukuni and others whom Casca has seen taking part in the defense of the village, but without any special distinction or authority.

Sakuvi and these others now dominated the conversation, together with a number of the women. From the few words he could understand, it seemed to Casca that the discussions were entirely concerned with crops and planting, the phases of the moon, fishing, building, the mundane matters that kept the village functioning day to day.

Semele was all questions, and as always, every question searched to the heart of the matter under discussion, his great, woolly head describing arcs of wonderment, puzzlement, comprehension, decision.

Casca watched this primitive monarch and wondered. Here in the chief's house, and at all the ceremonies he had seen, Semele always occupied a superior position. But only in the chief's house, it seemed, was he paramount. In the ordinary day to day life of the village, nobody paid him any deference, got out of his way, or even, it seemed to Casca, accorded him due respect.

If he wished to go fishing, the fishermen reluctantly made room for him in the canoe, making rude remarks about his size and usefulness, although he wielded his paddle as effortlessly and effectively as any. At the farm plots he hoed and raked and weeded as industriously as anybody. And around the village children were always trying to trip him up, or to creep up on him and take him by surprise, shrieking in delight when they succeeded and his mighty bulk would leave the ground in fright or in a well-feigned simulation of it. Mbolo came in for similar treatment, and responded in the same way.

Casca also noticed that everybody in the village brought to Semele's feet the slightest thing that bothered them. Anybody, it seemed, could stop the chief anywhere, anytime, and pour his troubles into his ear.

Semele would listen with his infinite patience, ask his perceptive questions, roll his great head. And often, Casca noticed, the supplicant would go away smiling, leaving Semele wearing a worried frown.

Not a job to be sought after, Casca thought, and he wondered how it had come to Semele.

"A job and a half mon, ain't it?" Sandy chuckled beside him, as if reading his thoughts.

"Not one for me, I'll be bound."

"Oy mon, not so loud. They've always an eye out for the next chief, and him who wants it least is him who gets it."

Casca was aware that the young Scot was smarter and more inquisitive than himself. "Is Semele the son of a chief, d'you know?"

"Of course he is."

"Ah," Casca said, thinking he understood.

"But his father, the old chief, was nae his sire."

"What are you talking about?" Casca demanded.

"Semele came here as a young man from one of the Fiji islands, and after a while the old chief moved him up, treating him like his own son until he was more or less his deputy, and eventually chief."

"So why did the old chief adopt him?"

"Lookit, mon, lookit. Excellence. Excellence and reluctance is what's looked for."

A twinge of his well-honed survival instinct surfaced in Casca. He was already a war chief. "But they wouldn't want to make a man chief against his will, would they?"

"Especially and only against your will, m'boy. And you're halfway there already, I'm thinking."

"Well, they'd be making a bad mistake," Casca grunted. "In the first place I sure don't intend to stay here, and I could never do Semele's job anyway. Sooner or later I'd fuck up if I tried it."

"No matter." Sandy laughed. "When you fuck up too badly, they'll eat you with all due respect. And sing your song for a hundred years."

The *bilo* of kava passed back and forth, and the discussions proceeded exactly as they had on the matter of warfare. Topics were raised and bandied back and forth, everybody who had an opinion expressing it. Semele asked penetrating questions, Mbolo made the occasional remark, and eventually Semele pulled together all the various threads, a decision was made, and a new topic was introduced.

Meanwhile the hollowed-out coconut shell never stopped moving from the bowl full of kava to one or another of the people and back to be refilled and passed again, the women only taking an occasional ceremonial *bilo* while the men consumed enormous quantities of the stuff.

Casca tried drinking more of it himself, having overcome his distaste for it and its mode of preparation, but apart from the vaguely pleasant numbness in his mouth and a faint tingling on his tongue, he could feel little effect.

It might have been that the attack of the Lakuvi had never taken place. In fact it seemed to Casca that to these people yesterday had already ceased to exist, that it had never existed in the first place.

The story of the day's events was down in the oral annals of the tribe. In both villages the story would be told from time to time. Because of Casca's role in the events, the story might well be still told in another hundred years.

But right now Watalo, the carpenter chief, was the one closest to Semele, and it was to him that the old man directed his penetrating questions, each reply being as thoughtfully considered as those in the warfare discussions. Casca had been told that the discussion was about the building of a new temple to replace the one destroyed in the hurricane that had brought the *Rangaroa* to the island. His agile linguistic ear put together the few words that he understood with the many that he didn't. It wasn't too hard for someone who had spent so many lifetimes learning so many different languages.

These people really loved to talk. The chief would roll out a beautifully sonorous question about, it seemed, roof thatch and the high plain where the grass for it grew and the distance to the village and the phases of the moon. And the carpenter chief would roll back the same question in slightly different words while he thought about it. And from all over the room, one after another, people would restate the question as they contributed thoughts or information, or just conversation on the topic.

Casca realized that this process of involving the whole village in the matter had also happened the night before the battle.

Suddenly Semele looked to him much less like a ruler and more like the chairman of a club.

Vivita had walked with Casca to the chief's house, as she usually did, and had sat somewhere near him throughout the evening. But now, he noticed, she seemed to have withdrawn, although without actually moving away. Numerous younger women were in the near vicinity, and it seemed to Casca that they were being more adventurously flirtatious with him than had happened recently.

When one stupendously pretty young girl indicated to him with her eyes that it was time for bed, Casca was taken by surprise and looked around.

Vivita sat within arm's reach, as did three or four other young lovelies. But Casca couldn't elicit any sort of response from any of them. Vivita returned his gaze without any apparent interest.

However, the silent contest had been decided. This beautiful young girl was clearly the winner, and it was clear that Casca could sleep with her, or perhaps by himself, but Vivita was not interested.

Only this time last night he'd wondered how he was going to get rid of Vivita, and now it seemed she had gotten rid of him. He was pretty sure that this little girl could not have taken him from the formidable Vivita had she wanted to hang on to him.

"Not too bad for a consolation prize," he muttered as he got up to leave with the luscious young woman.

She was tiny; her fuzzy head didn't even come up to Casca's armpit. And she was blacker than anybody he'd seen on the island. Undressed, even the area from her waist to her knees, protected from the sun most of the time by her grass skirt, was jet black.

Luisa was bewitchingly playful and had unlimited energy. Casca was almost relieved when, a little before dawn, she finally fell asleep.

But she was awake at the first beat of the drum, and within a few more beats was straddling Casca's body, nibbling at his ears and his neck, her prickly little pubis irritating Casca's penis to an unwanted erection.

When she eventually climbed off him, temporarily satisfied, Casca had time to wonder yet again what he could have done to offend Vivita.

Luisa served him a breakfast of crabmeat and breadfruit, and as Vivita usually did in the mornings, indicated that he should go to the chief's house to participate in the day's work.

CHAPTER ELEVEN

Casca had quite enjoyed his several day's of farming, but he was less than enthusiastic about much more of it. He had joined the Roman army nearly two thousand years earlier as a way out of spending his life plodding about a field, planting and weeding and harvesting.

At the chief's house he found that most of the crew of the *Rangaroa* were of the same mind. Most of them had gone to sea to escape the endless round of the farm.

"Maybe we could do some fishing," Liam suggested, and Larsen quickly asked the chief if they could do so.

Semele was quick to agree, and also hastened to point out that there were many other things to be done in the village, such as building and repairing houses and the defensive walls. Or if they preferred, they could stay at home and keep their women company, since there was no real reason for them to work at all.

Casca thought of spending the long, hot day on the grass mat with Luisa, and decided to go fishing.

Larsen sought out Watolo and with him went in search of a tree large enough to provide a new rudder.

Each of the *Rangaroa* crew was put into one of the twenty-man canoes with some of the natives, and they set out for the open sea.

By the time they got to the reef Casca's arms were aching, his legs trembling, and he found it necessary to concentrate every ounce of effort in order to keep time with the paddle strokes of the other men in his canoe. He looked with new respect at the smooth, rippling muscles of the fishermen.

Casca wondered if he would indeed have won the battle with the Lakuvi warrior if the arm-wrenching combat had gone on much longer.

He chuckled to himself. "Sure I would have. Takes a damned good arm to stand up to a .38 slug."

Once outside the reef they stopped paddling and drifted about on the deep water, hoping to catch some of the big fish that came to eat the smaller reef fish. Inside the reef other fishermen were fishing for these small fish, and way out to sea others in sail canoes were trying for the fast, active, big fish that bit at everything that moved near the surface of the water.

The sea teemed with fish, and by the end of the day almost every boat had a full catch. But Dukuni explained that sometimes the luck was not so good and between all the boats they might only take a few fish. And sometimes, too, there would be no fish at all for days and days on end.

Ulf and several others of the *Rangaroa*'s crew understood this all too well, and laughed to learn that the life of a professional fisherman was not all that different in the South Pacific than it was off the coast of Greenland or England.

The whole of the day's catch was spread out along the beach. There were small sharks, tuna, albacore, stingrays, barracuda, bass, groupers, snapper. Small boys fishing in the shallows had contributed tiny parrot fish and angelfish in a riot of colors, and the repulsive scorpion fish.

Chou Lui was delighted at the sight of these horrible little monsters, puffed up to three times their normal size, poisonous spines projecting. He protested vigorously when Kukuni went to discard them, and explained that he had learned in Japan how to prepare this poisonous fish as an exquisite delicacy.

There was an enormous feast in the village that night. It

seemed the generosity of the ocean must be celebrated by eating every morsel that could possibly be consumed, and the meal went on for hours. Casca had not seen anybody eat so much since the orgies of ancient Rome. One huge fish after another was brought in and consumed, while banana-leaf platters of smaller fish passed around and around. Nobody, it seemed, could leave until all the fish were eaten. Casca could see how the older people in the village attained such enormous size.

Ulf was amazed when he realized they were going to sit and eat until every last fish was consumed.

"Vy don't you just bickle de surplus?" he asked through a mouthful of fish.

"What is bickle?" Semele asked.

Ulf burst into laughter, spraying the air with half-chewed fish.

"Vot iss bickle? You don't know bickle?"

Semele shook his head.

"You put the fish in vinegar to keep it," Ulf mumbled through another mouthful.

"What is vinegar?" asked Dukuni.

"Oh, yeah, no vinegar," mumbled Ulf. "Well, you can use lemons."

"Lemons?"

"No lemons? Well, we can use saltpeter and water. Is too hard to explain. Tomorrow I show you." He crammed some more crab into his mouth.

Just when Casca was convinced that he could not possibly eat another mouthful and would have to commit the unpardonable social affront of refusing food, Chou Lui appeared from the direction of the cooking house.

He was bearing a huge banana leaf laden with fish, and was followed by two women with similar leaves. He delightedly explained that this was the poisonous scorpion fish, carefully cleaned and prepared as he had been taught in Japan. Casca thought that he could have cheerfully strangled him.

But the succulent fish soon made him change his mind.

Not only did he enjoy the fish, but it restimulated his appetite and he was able to continue with the feast.

At last every fish had been eaten, every bone picked clean, and attention was turned to the serious business of the night—the conversation as the *bilo* of kava passed around the room.

When Casca sought to divert the conversation to the topic that most concerned him—the likelihood of a renewed attack on the village, the response was delighted laughter.

If yesterday had already disappeared from the ken of these people, tomorrow was similarly out of sight.

The imminent threat of a murderous attack by Cakabau's musket-armed men had quite passed out of mind. The world was at peace, every belly in the village full. The gods were smiling. If there was a worthwhile topic of discussion, it could only surely be the building of the new temple.

All around the room one speaker after another dismissed Casca's concern and told and retold the story of the battle with the attackers from Lakuvi. Dukuni, the fisherman chief, told of the excellent use made of the captured Lakuvi canoes. Sonolo, the war chief, boasted of the number of war clubs abandoned by the fleeing enemy. Sakuvi, the farmer chief, predicted great crops of fruit and vegetables from the trees and plots of ground gained in the victory.

Each speaker retold the entire story of the battle, but not as if it were a real event that had happened only a few days ago. The battle was already a legend, and its tale was recounted like a fabled myth. Yesterday had passed out of existence, but the events remained—in the form of a great story.

One aspect of this impressed Casca. Each speaker took elaborate care to detail Casca's own role in the victory, to extol his bravery and good thinking, and to hold up to the audience the lesson that he had taught them in taking the enemy by surprise in his rear when the battle otherwise might not have even been joined.

Each story ended in gales of laughter as the speaker

came to his conclusion that never again, not under any circumstances, would the people of Lakuvi dare to attack the village of Navola.

It was Sandy who found a way to turn the discussion in the direction Casca sought. "Could Cakabau's raiders attack Navola without the assistance of Lakuvi?" he asked.

"Never," laughed Sonolo. "From Bau to Navola would take many many days by the fastest sail canoe, and even the biggest of Bau's sail canoes could not carry enough men to attack the village."

There was considerable discussion about the difficulties in Cakabau's way for an attack on the village without the assistance of the Lakuvi. Even Kini, veteran of the Bau attack on Vanua Levu and a very experienced seaman, considered it impossible.

"But surely," said Casca, "Cakabau would carry the day if he only brought six men with the muskets?"

"From inside our palisades we can laugh at his muskets," said Sonolo. "And once they are fired they are only puny clubs, are they not?"

"Yes," confirmed Kini, "if he wasted the use of his weapons on the walls we could then attack and the six men would be easy to defeat."

"These weapons only work once?" demanded Semele.

"Once in a long time," Kini answered, "then they must be cleaned and prepared for use again."

Single shot muzzle loaders, thought Casca.

Semele's mind was running in another direction. "How came Cakabau to your island of Vanua Levu?" he asked Kini.

"The trader, Savage, brought many of the men of Bau and their war canoes on his great sail canoe, a ship such as the *Rangaroa,* on which I came. Outside the reef Savage put the Bau canoes into the water and they came into the lagoon and attacked us on the beach, and then again at the village."

In previous kava discussions some in the tribe had grasped that with modern weapons, more than one man was often killed in battle. Now, Semele asked, "How many of your men did these fire weapons kill?"

"Three at first, on the beach, and we yielded. Then, at the village, when he demanded our men and we fought again, another four. And another who would have been better dead."

"Why kill so many?"

"It is the nature of the fire sticks," Kini answered unhappily. "And the men of Bau have gone mad for eating men. They cannot get enough. They eat men like we eat fish."

Semele looked disgusted, but pressed on with his questions. "Did they then eat all six men?"

"Yes, they did," Kini blurted out, still hurting at the memory. "They ate them in front of the village, before all of us." He groaned. "And then they used our women, there, on the ground before the village."

Semele waited a moment for Kini to recover himself. "So they took your women too?"

"Took them and fed them on their own men, and then used them. Used them disgracefully, and the women, after feasting on the men, permitted it and enjoyed it. And then they sent them back to us."

There was a long silence throughout the room. Finally Ateca spoke. "And did any of your women bear children to these men?"

"Oh, yes," Kini replied cheerfully. "We now have many Bau babies in the village. Many, many more than were killed."

There were nods and smiles all around the house at this happy news.

Semele returned to the heart of the matter. "So it is not good to fight him on the beach, and it is not good to fight him outside the walls. But we could not hide forever inside the walls, for the enemy outside would have food and water and we would not." He looked at Kini. "If he comes in Savage's great ship, could we attack him outside the reef?"

"Indeed, no," Kini replied. "Savage has these much greater weapons on his ship."

Semele closed his eyes and raised his great head toward the roof. Casca felt for the old man trying to find a way to fight such a powerful foe. He, too, closed his eyes and searched his memory and his imagination, but his mind stopped short at the thought of going up against muskets and cannon with wooden clubs.

Semele opened his eyes. "We must get some of these weapons."

Casca felt his little .38. He would use it in his own defense, but it could hardly be enough against six muskets, even if they were old muzzle loaders. He felt sure that Larsen had some muskets aboard, but was just as sure that Larsen would not part with them. No doubt he would use them if Cakabau's attack came before the *Rangaroa* sailed, but if there were only two or three muskets, they would hardly be enough either.

Kini spoke reluctantly. "In Levuka Savage will sell you a musket for ten men."

"One weapon, and he has six," said Mbolo.

Semele spoke with decision. "Then we shall give this Valangi ten times ten men and he will give us ten muskets. Then we shall see how these heroes of Bau will fight." He turned to Larsen. "Now that your ship is repaired, will you take our men in trade to Levuka?"

"The hell I will," Larsen snapped. "If I wanted to be a slaver, I'd have gone into the business before now, and I'd be as rich as Savage. No, Semele, I will not trade a cargo of slaves."

Semele closed his eyes and thought again for a long time, and at last asked. "Will you carry for us free men to Levuka?"

Larsen gave a short laugh. "Where they will sell themselves to Savage?"

"Yes."

Larsen looked at Liam and Sandy and the rest of his crew.

Ulf shrugged. "I wouldn't want to stand in their way."

For a moment Larsen thought of giving them his muskets, but he had already made the same calculation as Casca. He didn't have enough to make a difference, and it would mean that his ship would be defenseless against any pirates, or even wharf rats, who cared to attack her.

"All right," he said, "I'll take them, but I'll have no part in the trade. We'll carry them as free passengers on deck."

"Good." Semele nodded. "And now we must think of how to use these weapons. Where should we fight?"

Chou Lui spoke: "Excuse it, please, I am giving much thinking to this problem while I am preparing scorpion fish, and I remember words of great sage of my country, Sun Tzu. He say: 'Those skilled in war bring enemy to field of battle and not are brought there by him.'"

"Ah," said Semele, "this is wisdom. We will take the advice of your sage and bring the warriors of Bau to fight us here, where we are strongest."

The Chinese cook bowed. "Sun Tzu also say: 'Close to field of battle await enemy from afar; at rest await exhausted enemy; well-fed troops await hungry ones.'"

Semele smiled. "More great wisdom. The men of Bau will be weary with travel. We can harass them on the beach and give them no peace, but retire here so that they must pursue us."

Chou bowed again. "Sun Tzu say: 'In early morning spirits keen, in day spirits flag, in evening thoughts turn toward home.'"

"Aha." Chief Semele grunted. "Exactly. We shall bring the host of the enemy here with taunts, but during the day we will only harass them in hot sun while our host rests in the shade. And when they are tired and hungry and wanting to go home, then we shall attack."

Mbolo spoke to Chou. "What says your sage is the basis of war?"

Chou answered without a moment's hesitation. "All war is based on deception."

Sonolo's forehead creased in a worried frown. "Deception? What of morality, fortitude, courage, wisdom, preparedness?"

Chou clapped his hands and accepted the *bilo* of kava he was being offered. He drained the cup, clapped three times, intoned *"matha,"* and turned to Sonolo. "All of these are important. A wise and benevolent war chief who enjoys the confidence of his men will be strong in war; warriors who are well fed, prepared, rested, will fight well; strictness in discipline, fair reward and punishment will ensure that warriors will obey orders. All these are important, but they are but elements of war. The base of all war is deception."

Mbolo spoke to the others. "What do you think of this?"

Sakuvi spoke: "This sage is wise, and his advice is old and no doubt well tested. I think it is true."

"True?" Mbolo snapped. "How can it be true? That deception is stronger than truth? This is nonsense."

Silence spread quickly through the house. Even the chattering girls at the back of the room were quiet.

Finally Mbolo spoke slowly. "For us the truth is important. Truth is vital. Truth is paramount."

Sonolo nodded. "To go into battle against the truth is to ask for defeat."

There was another silence. Chou Lui bowed his head to his chest, his eyes closed. He sat there as if taking no further interest in the discussion.

Casca looked at the cook. He was himself a long-standing student of the Chinese master Sun Tzu and owed many of his victories to his advice. Yet he, too, knew what Sonolo meant about the need for respect for truth.

Chou's head snapped up and he spoke. "Let us consider the scorpion fish. It lies on the bottom of the sea and cannot be seen. Here is deception. But surely, too, there is truth, for is it not the true nature of this fish to lie thus waiting for its food?"

Several heads nodded in agreement, but the foreheads were creased in puzzlement.

"Comes a man seeking fish to eat, and the fish takes a deep breath of water, blows itself up to great size, projects its spines, floats on the surface so that it looks dead and repulsive and unfit to eat. More deception. And more of the true nature of the fish."

More heads nodded, but the puzzlement increased.

"But the man is not deceived. He is hungry. He takes the fish for he has heard that it is good to eat. He eats it and dies. His friends will never again eat this fish."

"The truth," Mbolo shouted, "see the truth."

"Yes," Chou Lui agreed, "the truth. The loathsome-looking fish is poisonous and none will eat it. But this truth is one more deception, for when this fish is properly cleaned it is safe to eat, delicious and fortifying. This fish survives by deception, yet always acts in truth."

Mbolo snapped his fingers. "I believe I see. Sonolo, do you see?"

Sonolo stroked his chin, scratched his shoulders, rubbed his belly. He pursed his lips and shook his head several times. "Perhaps," he said at last, "perhaps I do see. This is a new way to look at things, but perhaps I do see. Perhaps deceit can be of merit."

Semele rolled his head, raked his fingers through the thick, graying curls. "But we are strong in truth. In deception we are unskilled. How shall we learn? Who will teach us?"

Casca looked carefully at the floor. Larsen had told him that all the damage from the hurricane had been repaired and that he was ready to sail.

"Not me, old chief," he muttered to himself. "I intend to be well gone from here before Cakabau attacks."

CHAPTER TWELVE

That night, somehow, none of the young lovelies attempted to seduce Casca, and Vivita went home with him as if she had never done otherwise. He assumed that she had her own, probably physiological, reasons for staying away for a few nights, and so had allowed some of the other young women at the village to keep him company. In the morning he was surprised at how pleased he was to awake and find her ugly face next to his.

When Casca got to the chief's house he found that there was to be no work in the village that day. Instead all the strongest, bravest men in the village were to compete for the honor of being sold in Levuka in trade for the muskets that would be used to defend the village against Cakabau.

Casca and the crew of the *Rangaroa* were invited to compete in the games, but to a man they found a seven-year contract to work under the whip on Australia's sugar fields an unattractive prospect, and all of them declined to compete.

Casca was irritated by the whole idea of men competing to sell themselves into slavery, no matter how worthy the cause, and was delighted when Vivita suggested that they spend the day visiting her family in the village where she had been born.

They climbed the mountain, passing the recently acquired lands of the Lakuvi, and then descended into the enemy village.

Casca had not understood that Vivita had been born a mortal enemy of the Navola tribe, and had not realized that this was the village she had intended to visit. He was much reassured by the feel of the .38 in his pocket.

They were greeted rapturously. Vivita had been a favorite daughter of the village before her capture in a raid by the Navola men, and Casca was a famous hero.

All activity in the village ceased, and they sat in the chief's house and drank kava and feasted and talked until late into the night.

All the men wanted to sit close to Casca, and the women, it seemed, could not hear enough of Vivita's life amongst the enemy. Three or four young girls were especially keen to hear of life in the Navola village, and Casca learned that these girls were Navola who had been captured by the Lakuvi as Vivita had been taken by the Navola.

They seemed as happy to be captives in the enemy household as Vivita was in the Navola village, and it appeared to Casca that they could probably leave if they so wished and walk back across the mountain to their original homes.

But he was really surprised to meet two young warriors, one a few years younger than he himself appeared to be, the other not much more than a boy. These were men of the Navola who had seen and been captivated by Lakuvi women but had been unsuccessful in their attempts at capturing them, and so had themselves changed villages.

More and more it seemed to Casca that the historical enmity between these two villages was a great convenience to both peoples. It kept them sufficiently apart so that each maintained its identity, and provided the rationale for the occasional much enjoyed wars and even more enjoyable cannibal feasts and orgies that followed them. And the raids to capture enemy women, together with the occasional voluntary intermarriage and the hospitality to visitors, ensured that neither village became inbred.

He was musing on this matter in the soft afterglow of

many cups of kava when he realized that several young women were sitting close by him while Vivita, though still alongside, seemed remote.

He sat comfortably on his haunches and accepted another *bilo* of kava while he waited interestedly to see which of these young lovelies was to succeed in winning him for the night.

For the first time Casca felt something of what the islanders liked so much about kava. The pleasant, faintly numbing sensation that he felt in his lips and gums and tongue now seemed to spread throughout his body, so that he felt pleasantly at ease and unconcerned with the petty details of existence. An effect, he thought, perhaps somewhere between fine cognac and hashish, yet quite unlike either.

Life here in these cannibal isles was undeniably pleasant, and the drug's effect seemed to alert him to this pleasantness and to confirm it to himself. He wondered why this aspect of kava had not been apparent to him earlier, and assumed that the drug worked by some process of accumulation within the body.

Amidst all this pleasantness there were these lovely ladies who were playing some sort of game which he couldn't see or hear, and certainly couldn't understand, but in which he knew that he was the prize. When the game was over he found that he had been won by Lalonia, the prettiest of the girls, a lusty, busty belle of perhaps sixteen years.

As they crossed the village square he looked at her in the moonlight and wondered if he had played any part in the game. Perhaps, he thought, they kept some sort of score of his glances, body movements, sighs, gestures. Perhaps. Perhaps, too, he was not even in the game, but merely a toy to be won and played with for the night and discarded in the morning. He decided he must question Sandy about it. The canny young Scot had surely found out how the game worked.

Lalonia took him to a small empty hut, freshly swept

clean, with a sleeping mat in a corner, fruits and coconuts beside it.

It must have been the effect of the kava. Their lovemaking seemed to go on forever. He awoke and was completely surprised to find Vivita beside him.

They lingered in the enemy village for several days, and each night Casca went to bed with a different woman, to wake each morning with Vivita. He guessed there was some matter of protocol and courtesy involved. As a visitor, and more, a celebrity, he was entitled to all the hospitality the village could offer. And Vivita yielded her place to those young girls whose role it was to extend a part of that hospitality.

He also thought that perhaps his prowess as a warrior was held to be of value in improving the bloodline of the tribe, and that one or more of these young women might hope to bear his child. Perhaps this was even the reason Vivita had suggested the visit.

Vivita, he guessed, returned to his mat before dawn each morning to assert her marital rights and to make it clear that Casca would not be staying in the village with any of these women.

Casca also assumed that she herself spent the greater part of the night with another man, since she didn't bother making love with him, which was most unusual for her.

Whatever the reasons for the arrangement, it suited Casca very well, and it came as a surprise to him when one morning Vivita jerked her head in the direction of the Navola village to indicate that it was time to return.

With only the briefest of good-byes they left the village where Vivita had been born and grew to womanhood, and set out for the village of her sworn enemies, where she lived placidly and happily.

They arrived back at the village to find that the *Rangaroa* had sailed, bearing away on her decks a hundred of the best men of the village to be sold as slaves in the marketplace at Levuka, the capital of Cakabau's new kingdom of Fiji.

Casca was more than a little unhappy when he learned

that the *Rangaroa* had sailed without him, without even giving him a chance to say farewell to the crew, who had become such good friends. But then, he had farewelled enough ships, said good-bye to enough friends. He was also unhappy to find himself marooned on the island. If ever another merchant ship were to call at the island, it was likely to be the slaver Savage, or Boyd or Bentley, or some other Australian just as bad.

He was especially uneasy about the fact that Sonolo had set out to buy the muskets on which his own liberty might depend without consulting with him. To be sure, any muskets would do, and there would not be many choices offered in the small town of Levuka. But the feeling of unease persisted.

Casca didn't know that in addition Semele had neglected to tell him that the *Rangaroa* might be returning. He wanted Casca's full attention given to Cakabau's imminent attack.

CHAPTER THIRTEEN

The games had lasted all day and much of the night, and included every test of strength, agility, skill, and courage that the mind of man could conceive using trees and mountains and coral reefs and underwater caves, pounding surf, calm lagoon waters, sharks and stingrays.

The drums called the whole village to the square, and the first event started then and there.

At one corner stood the great pole of the ruined temple, surrounded by its ruins and carved gods. At a signal from Semele every young man in the village raced for the pole, elbowing, pushing each other out of the way, tripping each other up, fighting to be first to get to the pole. One man might knock down half a dozen others, but would only just begin his climb when he would be dragged down and another would take his place, only to be dragged down in his turn.

Then there were three or four men on the pole, each trying to drag down the man above him and kick away those below him. One made it halfway up, to be seized from below by two others, so that all three crashed heavily to the ground.

Eventually one man did make it to the top, but fell when he attempted to stand erect. And at last there was one man standing on the forty-foot pole, kicking away the arms that tried to clutch at his legs and bring him crashing to the ground.

The drum sounded, and everybody cheered the one who had earned the right to be enslaved.

Another proved his worth by ducking, weaving, running around the square without being hit by any of the stones, sticks, fruit, and coconuts thrown by the villagers. The several contestants knocked unconscious were laid out alongside the groaning wrecks from the pole-climbing contest.

A little later in the morning Semele's son qualified for the trip to Australia by capturing a small shark with his bare hands. The feat was accomplished by diving onto the shark from a canoe, grasping it about the body, and hurling it into the boat. None of the other contestants managed to catch one, and miraculously none lost an arm or a leg to the several enraged sharks that they were after.

Spearing a stingray and maneuvering it in its death throes to the shore by riding on its back, got another the right to end his life cutting sugarcane under the lash.

One of Mbolo's sons qualified by diving on the reef, staying down longer than anybody else, and coming up with the biggest basket of lobsters.

The biggest rock that could be found was rolled to the edge of the square. A contestant carried it until he collapsed in exhaustion. The next contestant carried it back to and beyond his starting point. Another managed to carry it farther, then another a little farther, until another slave was finally chosen.

The best wrestlers and runners and swimmers were selected. Men slapped each other's faces until one or the other collapsed. Some walked into the fires and stood on the hot stones amongst the coals until all others had fled the heat or collapsed.

Men knotted vines about their ankles to dive from the top of the temple pole, the winner being the one who best calculated the length and spring of the vines so that they stopped him just short of the ground. Those who cut their vines too short lost the contest. Those who cut them too long would never be any use as slaves, anyway, nor as much of anything else.

By the end of the day the cream of the manhood of the village had been selected for slavery; however, two were dead, some more dying, and a score more gravely injured.

CHAPTER FOURTEEN

Larsen had waited two days in the hope that Casca would return, but he'd already lost a great deal of time and was anxious to get the *Rangaroa* to Levuka, unload her cargo from San Francisco, and get on his way to Sydney. And the trading of the slaves grew more urgent, too, since the raid from Bau might happen any day.

Larsen had mentioned to Semele that he would sail as soon as Casca returned.

The old chief looked at him shrewdly. "Surely you will sail back in this direction?"

"Yes," Larsen answered. "I have cargo to Sidney, and I intend to load wool there for San Francisco."

"Then you could leave Casca here with us and collect him on your return."

Larsen knew what the sly chief was up to. "Well, I guess I could, but I'm not sure Casca would like it. In addition I can give no guarantee that I can find this island again. It is uncharted and we may not be so lucky finding it a second time."

Semele laughed. "Do not worry. We will make sure that Casca is kept happy. He can be of great help to us in this coming fight with Cakabau. And if you do not find our island again, another ship will eventually come."

Larsen had hesitated. Certainly he was heavily in debt

to these islands. And his rugged passenger could certainly find passage on any ship that pulled in here.

Watolo, the carpenter chief, and Dukuni, the fisherman chief, and their men had worked mightily with his crew to repair the *Rangaroa*.

A new rudder had been hewn from a log that had been intended for a canoe, and the villagers had worked hard and long to help the ship's crew set it in place. They had hauled the ship onto the beach at high tide and maneuvered her around with lines tied to their canoes and to the shore, until at low tide she lay like a great beached whale, her side high and dry in the air.

The crew and the villagers worked for many days, stripping the barnacles from the hull and then recaulking every seam. Then the huge rudder was carried out into the sea and secured to the stern.

At the next high tide the ship was laid over the other way and the entire process repeated while she lay on her other side, every fastening being replaced so that the new rudder was as sound and secure as when the ship was first launched.

Then the decks were scoured and recaulked, until at last the *Rangaroa* was ready for sea.

There being no reason to tarry longer on the island, since every day wasted meant a loss for Larsen and the whole crew, he asked Ulf about Casca.

The dour Greenlander was checking the lines to the new rudder. "Leave him," he grunted, not even looking up.

The fastest of the village's sail canoes was loaded aboard the *Rangaroa,* and with the hundred prospective slaves on deck she shook out her sails and departed.

In two days they were in Levuka, and Larsen and the others were surprised at the English city they found on the small tropical island.

The wharves were as well built as any in San Francisco, and ships were tied up from all over the world. There were three masted deepwatermen out of Bremen and Antwerp and London, carrying pots and pans, iron stoves, horseshoes, anvils and axes, shotguns and muskets, and a thousand items from Europe to ease the life of the men and women who were establishing homes in the newest British colony.

From America, too, there were ships with farm tools and bicycles, buggies and drays, elegant clocks from New England, pocket knives and tableware from Pennsylvania.

There was a junk from China unloading silks and satins, soaps and perfumes, and fine porcelains. They would carry back bêche-de-mer and sandalwood and coconut oil and sharks' fins.

And there were the slavers, known as blackbirders, mostly small, fast schooners similar to the *Rangaroa*. They were all clustered together on the western edge of the harbor, away from the main trading places and close by the offices of the Colonial Sugar Refinery Company.

The company itself did not deal in slaves, but arranged contracts for its Australian planters. Indeed, through shrewd manipulation of the letter of the law, blackbirding was not slavery but recruiting of indentured labor.

Each slave signed a contract, which, of course, he could not read. Nor was he offered the alternative of declining to sign. In return for the signature on the contract his recruiter received a cash payment that varied according to the slave's appearance, strength, and skills. Close by the CSR Company's offices there was a stockyard where the blackbirds were penned and awaiting valuation, and an auction block where their lives and liberties were hammered down to the highest bidder.

But the auctioneer didn't say "sold" as the hammer fell. That would make it slavery, and the British Empire had outlawed slavery long before the United States had.

As he auctioneer brought the bidding to a close with a rap of his hammer he said: "Indentured by a contract of seven years to work as directed in the Colony of New South Wales, at the rate of threepence a day and all found."

"All found" meant one bowl of rice a day. Anything else the slave might want—a piece of meat, some tobacco, a hat for shelter from the blazing tropical sun, a pair of pants, or the use of a woman—he would have to buy from the company store out of his three pennies a day.

There was no pay for Sundays, but there was a day's work all the same—building, maintaining, and furnishing the Methodist church and its parsonage, which the company maintained on each of its properties for the good of the heathen souls of its indentured labor.

At the end of his seven years under the lash, if the blackbird was one of the few who survived, the CSR Company paymaster would present him with an account that showed how he had spent his three pennies a day and how much more he was in debt to the company.

The slave could not read the account nor add up its figures, any more than he could understand the new seven-year contract he was forced to sign to pay off his accumulated debts.

And in the House of Lords in London, learned gentlemen made speeches congratulating each other on the splendid progress of the Colony of New South Wales, which was prospering without need of the evils of slavery, an example to all the world thanks to the practical and Christian system of indenture which had replaced the convict system.

The small city of Levuka was laid out neatly around the harbor and up into the foothills of the mountains. The swampland had been drained and the waters diverted through a pleasantly meandering canal. The elegant ladies of the city, wives of the administrators of the colonial government and of the sugar company officers, promenaded the canal footwalls under their parasols, stopping to meet and chat at one or another of the pretty little bridges. There were several gentlemen's clubs, numerous churches, and a freemasons' lodge.

The blackened ruins of the U.S. consul's residence stood out starkly against the green of the jungle behind it. No amount of inquiry could elicit for Larsen any explanation for the existence of a U.S. consulate in a city whose only real business was slavery.

But the people of Fiji had looked at the biggest and the

best house in the city, had come to their own conclusions about the activities of the consul, and burned his mansion to the ground.

The U.S. government was outraged, and the president demanded that Cakabau pay compensation of ten thousand U.S. dollars, about a hundred times what the house had cost to build and roughly ten thousand times all the U.S. dollars in Fiji.

But the cannibal king was just starting to enjoy his monarchy, and did not relish the implied threat that the U.S. might depose him and set up a democracy in his islands.

So Cakabau had sought around for a village small enough to subdue easily but large enough to provide the number of slaves needed to justify a recruitment fee of ten thousand U.S. dollars. Navola filled the bill nicely, was sufficiently far away to minimize any repercussions, and moreover was on an uncharted island and therefore officially did not exist.

Larsen refused to tie up the *Rangaroa* alongside the blackbirders, arguing with the harbormaster that he carried free men, not blackbirds. That they had chosen to sell themselves was not his concern, and he wanted no part of it. He unloaded the sail canoe that would carry Sonolo and the muskets back to Navola, and it bobbed on the tide alongside the *Rangaroa*. Before leaving Navola he had insisted that the islanders not offer themselves to the sugar company until after the *Rangaroa* had sailed.

His ship had lost many weeks of valuable time, and Larsen pushed his crew and the local stevedores to turn the ship around in only two days, working late into the night with the aid of kerosene lamps.

Sonolo and the others farewelled the *Rangaroa* from the wharf, then walked to the CSR Company's offices, where the selected hundred men signed their contracts and Sonolo collected the recruitment fee.

That same afternoon the hundred sailed for the Tweed River in New South Wales, locked in the hold of Captain Bentley's famous blackbird schooner *Albatross*.

On the next morning's tide Sonolo and his crew set out for Navola, carrying ten brand-new Bonehill muskets.

CHAPTER FIFTEEN

Casca had long since decided against any attempt at enslaving the cheerful, happy, essentially harmless people of Navola, or their neighbors in Lakuvi.

But he urgently needed to make some money, and slaving had been his purpose in coming to these islands. Nor, in the time that he had been in the Pacific islands, had he seen any prospect of any other way of turning a sizable penny. He certainly had none of Larsen's revulsion for the trade. He'd been a slave himself more than once, and had owned slaves without number. As far as he could see, the practice of slaving was as much a part of the human race as warfare or thievery or deception. He was as happy to be a slaver as he was to fight, steal, or deceive, as circumstances might demand.

But stranded on the most westward of the Cannibal Isles, way outside any shipping lanes and without arms, men, or a ship, he could not see how he was to accomplish the trick of obtaining such a cargo and getting it to Australia.

Cakabau's threatened raid seemed to present the nearest thing he was likely to find to an opportunity. If the slaver, Savage, carried the raiders to Navola in his ship, as seemed likely, then there was a chance to defeat Cakabau, capture his men, seize the ship, and sail it to Australia.

The plan had a few ragged edges, but for the moment nothing else presented itself, so Casca continued to think along these lines.

One considerable difficulty was legality. Everything he'd heard convinced him that the coterie of one-time thieves and forgers who ran Australia liked everything to be scrupulously legal, which was what accounted for slaves being processed through the recruitment center in Levuka rather than being shipped direct from capture to the Tweed River; legality, and the temper of the Irish-slaves who made up the alternative labor force of Australia.

The Paddys, who themselves had been similarly dragged in chains from their homes in Ireland, deeply resented the efforts of the landowners to import slaves while they were seeking work for pay. Whenever they could, they attacked slaver ships as they docked, overpowering the authorities by the sheer fury of their unarmed assault and freeing the blackbirds, who would run away and join the bush tribes of aboriginals.

The planters, the slavers, and the CSR Company would all be badly out of pocket, and lacked any legal base for the pursuit of their escaped workers. So the company insisted that the indenture contracts be signed in another, suitably respectable British colony prior to the labor's arrival in Australia. The company could then send the New South Wales Police Force to recover their indentured workers at the public's expense.

Even the now free Paddys had never been referred to as slaves, although doomed to work under the lash. Through another ingenious manipulation of the letter of the law under the system known as British Justice, they were known as convicts. Which meant that they had been convicted—usually tried and found guilty of some serious offense, such as snaring a hare on the lands that their families had owned for the past thousand years but were now the property of the English judge trying them. These offenses, together with others—such as the wearing of the green or the poaching of a trout from his Lordship's stream—merited hanging, and the English judges were liberal in handing down death sentences.

A merciful British government would then commute these sentences to a life of penal servitude in the police colony of New South Wales.

The hapless Irish, with their firm belief in an eternity of paradise hereafter, and having been economically denied even the prospect of sin, would have preferred to escape their sorry plight at the end of a rope, but the option was never extended.

In the police colony they were allocated to slave either on government works or for landowners such as Sir Joseph Banks, the private owner of Cuba, founder of the Royal Society and the man who had sent Bligh and the *Bounty* to Tahiti on an errand to carry breadfruit seedlings at public expense to Cuba to feed his African slaves.

Australia was a fair bit larger than Cuba, and Sir Joseph had found it expedient to share its ownership with a few dozen or so cronies and relatives.

After the mutiny against Bligh the control of the penal colony was seized by the warders—the New South Wales Corps—military criminals who had been given the choice of hanging in England for crimes such as cowardice, desertion, and forgery, or acting as screws in New South Wales. Once Bligh was deposed, they established the world's first police state, as proclaimed in the *Government Gazette* of the day, along with a virtually free issue of rum similarly proclaimed, which kept the entire population rotten drunk for some weeks, ensuring that the coup went unresisted and virtually unnoticed.

The convict slave who cranked the press for the *Gazette* that falsely accused Governor Bligh of treason and announced the rum issue, received as his reward the right to run the colony's only newspaper. The new masters of the colony gave him the *Government Gazette* printing press, and the Sydney *Daily Times* was born.

By 1867 affairs in the colony had been so nicely managed that in London Sir Warwick Fatfeld, Chairman of the Bank of New South Wales, would leave the Threadneedle

Street boardroom of the bank and stroll to the House of
Lords, where he could make a pretty speech congratulating
his cousin—the chairman of the Colonial Sugar Refinery
Company of New South Wales—on his splendid achievement in providing cheap and plentiful sugar for the tables
of the Empire without the necessity of indulging in the
disgusting and un-Christian practice of slavery.

At their gentlemen's club he had already privately con-
gratulated his cousin on the splendid contribution the CSR
Company had made to the family coffers.

Another cousin, the saintly and venerable Bishop Forth-
dike, of the Angelican Church of New South Wales but
conveniently pensioned off to London where he could
enjoy the cricket, would rise in his seat in the same exalted
chamber to confirm that his colleague, the Right Reverend
Morris Ormond, Moderator General of the Methodist
Church in Australia—but, of course, being Methodist, not
a member of the House of Lords—had told him of the
happy lives the indentured Fijians enjoyed on the New
South Wales sugar fields, of their devotion to their church,
and the selfless way they devoted their Sundays to working
on their churches and on their pastors' houses and to tending the crops of the pastors and their families.

A month later, in Sydney, Sir James Fatfeld would run
an editorial in the family newspaper, the Sydney *Daily
Times*, extolling the speech his brother Sir Warwick had
made in the Lords and calling for his further well-merited
advancement and preferment in the peerage of the British
Empire.

CHAPTER SIXTEEN

The return of Sonolo's canoe with its cargo of ten muskets was an occasion for great rejoicing in the village. Semele, Mbolo, and Casca each rode in the stern of a twenty-man canoe to greet Sonolo at the opening in the reef, while every other craft in the village hung back a little behind them.

The three canoes traveled abreast from the shore, Semele and Mbolo pulling as lustily on their paddles as Casca was on his. If any one of the three was tired when they got to the reef, it was Casca, and he resolved once again that he must spend more time in the canoes. It irked him to see these old men plying their paddles so effortlessly when he was starting to tire.

Sonolo dropped his sail as soon as he had negotiated the opening to the reef, and lines of plaited vines were passed aboard to be taken up by the three canoes. The sixty men ceremoniously towed the sail canoe to the beach below the village, and where every man, woman, and child who could not fit into one of the boats waited.

The three canoes ran up onto the beach and a hundred hands seized the lines to haul the sail canoe ashore. Semele, Mbolo, and Casca took up positions on the beach, and the single crate containing the guns was placed before them with great ceremony. Casca was impatient to inspect the contents, but was forced to sit in silence while Sonolo told the entire story of his voyage from Levuka to the island. The great kava bowl was brought from the chief's house, the whale's tooth on its long rope placed at Sonolo's feet, and he was offered the first *bilo* of kava.

The second *bilo* was offered to the crate, and Mbolo clapped in acceptance on its behalf, took the *bilo* and poured it over the crate, clapped his hands three times, intoned *"matha,"* and returned the cup.

Now, thought Casca, but he was deceived. The *bilo* passed next to Semele, then to Mbolo, then to himself, and then it seemed around the entire population of the village. Although it was not yet noon, Casca began to wonder if he would get to see the guns by daylight.

Eventually, when some protocol that Casca could not even guess at had been satisfied, Sonolo shouldered the crate and the whole village headed for the chief's house.

Casca looked around for a keg of gunpowder, and not seeing one, began to feel very uneasy.

At the chief's house the whole procedure was repeated again, this time Casca noting that his own importance had somehow been subtly diminished, although only very slightly.

"The hell with rank," he muttered to himself, "just so long as he got the full works."

But still Casca had to wait.

Sonolo now went into a detailed description of the island of Ovalau as seen from the sea when he approached it on the deck of the *Rangaroa*. This was followed by an immensely more detailed description of the town of Levuka.

In spite of his impatience Casca was moved to admiration. A trained engineer surveyor in Caesar's legions could not have done better, could not even have done as well.

Sonolo described the arc of buildings that spanned the waterfront, and the British fort that guarded the harbor, although most of its guns were trained inland as a precaution against insurrection; Cakabau's white palace with its flag flying, a miniature replica, it seemed to Casca, of

Buckingham Palace in London, where the King of England lived. Sonolo described the many ships that jammed the roads in the harbor, the dress of their seamen, and the strange cargoes he saw unloaded.

He explained his interview with the CSR Company agent, the signing of the contracts, and then, to Casca's complete astonishment, he recounted the auctioning of each of the hundred men, ending each individual tale with the amount for which each man was sold.

As he got to this piece of information everybody in the room would cheer at the figure, and then there would be some spirited conversation as all of the sold man's most intimate friends confirmed that he was well worth the price.

These prices ranged between three and ten pounds, amounts which meant nothing to the islanders, but they cheered just the same. But to Casca the sums indicated that human flesh was indeed cheap in these parts. Assuming that the plantation owner also had to pay Captain Bentley a pound or two for the transportation of his men, he would be buying his slaves for less than fifty American dollars each.

"Too damned cheap," he muttered to himself, and quickly realized that the company agent had probably organized a closed auction to swindle Sonolo of the true price of his tribesmen.

As far as Casca could tell, Sonolo had been similarly swindled in the price of the muskets, as almost all of the money received for the men had apparently gone to their purchase.

At last, and after much more ceremony, the crate was opened, and Casca was relieved to see that they were first class, muzzle-loading, cap and ball muskets made by Bonehill, one of the best English gunsmiths. He was even more relieved to see that the crate contained ramrods, a plentiful supply of shot and caps, and ten powder horns.

Sonolo set up a demonstration of the power of the weapons. He used a number of men to represent the logs of the outer palisade of the village, and set up his musketeers behind them. Other men representing Cakabau's warriors took up some of the muskets and went through a dumb show of expending their charges uselessly on the stockade logs, each of which reacted comically by clutching at himself as if hit with something like a flying stone, while the defending musketeers crouching behind him laughed lustily.

Then the men with the muskets came out from cover and gleefully dispatched Cakabau's men, each of whom clutched at himself somewhere to indicate that he had been hit.

They clearly had no real idea of the efficacy of gunfire, as the defenders also made great show of clubbing the shot men, who presumably were merely dazed by musket balls through the stomach, ribs, eyes, genitals.

Casca enjoyed the show immensely, and so did everybody else. But Sonolo was not finished.

At a signal his crewmen produced a number of other crates, which held all manner of trade goods. There were cheap, gaudy lengths of cotton from Manchester, vastly inferior in quality and design to the tapa cloth made on the island; mirrors, beads, some shovels and hoes and other farming tools; a few axes and several knives.

The goods were gleefully passed from hand to hand around the room, and within a few minutes there was blood all over everything as one after another they cut themselves on the sharp edges of the steel tools. It didn't at all dampen their enthusiasm or spoil their fun but rather added to it, each new wound being greeted with shrieks of delighted laughter from both victim and those around him.

Sonolo had one more surprise, and at first Casca was as delighted as anybody to see it. His crew men dragged in one more large crate and opened it to reveal several dozen bottles of Scotch whiskey.

The first bottle was opened, poured a cupful at a time into the *bilo,* and passed back and forth as if it were kava. Casca was the fourth to be treated, and downed the several ounces of whiskey at a gulp, as was the custom with kava.

He clapped his hands happily as he passed back the *bilo,* saying *"matha,"* it is empty, with gusto.

But somewhere along the line the ceremonial distribution of the liquor faltered, and soon bottles were being opened all over the house and passed from hand to hand, everybody gulping the whiskey greedily from the neck of the bottle.

Semele saw what was happening and had the good sense to quickly secure half a dozen bottles for the chiefs. Indeed, Casca wound up with a bottle to himself, which suited him very well.

It was Casca's first drink since leaving the railroad camp many months earlier, and he savored each mouthful, pleasurably feeling it warming his gut all the way down and then rising back up to his brain. By the time he had consumed about a quarter of the bottle he was starting to feel pretty good.

A number of the villagers were even more enthusiastic, and quite unaccustomed to the firewater, were soon reeling more or less senselessly about the room, giggling and stumbling and having a great time.

Sonolo especially was very quickly the worse for the liquor, and Casca reflected what a stroke of luck it was that the man's sense of duty had brought him home before he had opened the case. Had he done so on Ovalau, it was clear the muskets would never have left that island.

Around the room the liquor was taking more and more effect. The young girls were all very quickly affected, and left the back of the room to dance lewdly before the chiefs. Several young men jumped up to dance with them, the dance quickly degenerating into hugging and fondling. The normally modestly behaved girls responded willingly to the pawing, and several couples only managed to make it outside through the intervention of the older women, before coupling.

But soon some of the older women were up there dancing, too, and being pawed, and in turn dragged off.

Casca was amused and highly entertained. Numerous girls danced before him and tried to drag him to his feet, in spite of Vivita's manifest disapproval. But Casca was in no mood for coupling with a drunk. He was enjoying his first drink in many months and was content to sip away at his bottle and be entertained by the antics going on around him.

Semele and Mbolo seemed to have the same idea, and so did their women. Ateca and Duana sat alongside their men, talking to Setole, Mbolo's sister, and taking an occasional appreciative sip from their bottles, but clearly with no intention of getting drunk. Casca was pleased (he couldn't quite understand why) to see that Vivita, too, behaved in this dignified, chief's wife fashion.

Most of the chiefs' wives were similarly abstemious, and by no means due to their men's example. All of the minor chiefs were making pigs of themselves, like Sonolo.

Sakuvi, the farmer chief, a quiet, dignified man, became surly and glowered at Sonolo. Casca had been told that the farmer was a formidable warrior who had fought with considerable distinction in many battles throughout his life. It seemed now that the firewater had brought out some deep-seated resentment toward the warrior chief.

Sonolo sensed Sakuvi's temperament and reacted similarly, the two sneering and snarling at each other, striking aggressive poses in which they mimicked and ridiculed each other.

Casca had seen a thousand situations like this result in murderous fights, and he glanced at Semele, expecting the wise old man to ameliorate the situation. But either he, too, had been affected by the alcohol, or possibly a fight between chiefs was nobody's business but their own.

Casca was furious. The battle with Cakabau's force might be only days away, could happen tomorrow, and if the men from Bau arrived in force, the village would not have one man too many for its defense. Yet here were perhaps the two best warriors about to try and kill each other. His anger grew at his powerlessness. Hell, he was Casca, the war chief, but his limited knowledge of the customs and the language made him a powerless onlooker.

Sakuvi and Sonolo were now quite close, within arm's

reach of each other, muttering insults, sneering, snarling, but so drunk that much of what they said was meaningless mumbling, their threatening poses becoming absurd as one or the other of them would stumble and almost fall.

Suddenly they were grappling. For the moment their drunkenness was overcome by their exertion as each strained for the advantage.

To Casca it was pretty poor wrestling. There were no recognizable holds or subtle use of leverage, but merely a push and pull dispute between two very strong men.

But what the contest lacked in sophistication was made up for in drunken malice. In a moment the two were on the ground, kicking, biting, punching, clawing at each other. Sakuvi grabbed Sonolo by the balls, Sonolo butted him heavily in the face, and he let go. Sonolo brought up his knee to catch Sakuvi in the same place, and he doubled up in pain. Then Sonolo had him in a strangle hold, Sakuvi too drunk and too hurt to get out of it.

Sakuvi's eyes bulged from his head, his tongue protruded; there was little chance that Sonolo could break the great, columnar neck, but he could certainly crush the windpipe and keep it closed.

Which is just what happened. The primitive hold worked for Sonolo, his opponent drunkenly incapable of countering it. Very soon Sonolo was strangling a corpse, too drunk to realize that the fight was over.

And it wasn't. All over the house new fights were breaking out as partisans of the two chiefs attacked each other. And then people were attacking each other for no reason at all.

Casca saw a number of men who were not drunk striving to break up the fights and only succeeding in getting involved in them.

The axes and knives, forgotten while everybody was drinking peaceably, now began to appear. One shambling, stumbling drunk with an axe falling about in every direction, flailing with it as he went, slicing off an ear here, a hand there, a few fingers somewhere else, didn't even realize what he was doing. People were stabbing each other, gouging out eyes, hacking off arms and legs. Their nervous systems, desensitized by the unaccustomed dose of the second most powerful anesthetic known, caused them to be not only unaware of the extent of their own injuries, but totally disinterested in the pain they were inflicting. The entire room was one gigantic bloodbath.

Casca looked at Semele and Mbolo, but neither of the big chiefs made a move.

Then Ateca was on her feet, Duana beside her, each of the old women with one of the ceremonial clubs in hand.

They charged into the thick of the fighting, laying to left and right as they went, every swing connecting with a head, every head crashing to the ground.

Vivita, Setole, and some of the other chiefs' wives grabbed clubs, too, and followed. Casca watched, half astonished, half amused.

Vivita smashed her club into the back of the head in front of her and the body fell, the opponent left facing Vivita with an axe in his hand. He raised it, but started back at the fury in the woman's face, and that was the last he knew for a long time as her club crushed his nose into a pulp.

In a few minutes there was nobody standing but the women and a handful of men who were not hopelessly drunk and had helped in separating the last of the brawlers.

The evening's celebrations were very definitely over.

Casca picked up what was left of his bottle of whiskey and headed for his hut.

CHAPTER SEVENTEEN

Casca lay on his grass mat, looking into the darkness, taking an occasional sip of his whiskey and doing some bloody-minded thinking.

If Cakabau were to attack on the morrow, or anytime within the next few days—while half the village was recovering from its wounds—he would certainly be victorious.

Clearly Sonolo had no real idea of how to use the muskets. Ten musketeers and at least ten replacements must be trained to use the weapons. They would have to learn how to load the charge of powder, then the wad, ram home the ball, another wad, then the firing cap. Then they would have to learn how to aim, how to fire without losing aim, and how to reload. For any hope of real effectiveness they should also know how to dismantle, clean, and reassemble the guns.

Perhaps he could manage to train ten good men in a day—if Sonolo would let him. After the events of this evening he no longer had the same confidence in his fellow war chief. If he had so little self-control that he could be provoked into killing another chief over a slight to his role as war chief, how would he react when Casca attempted to take charge of the muskets?

And what if Cakabau now had more than the six muskets? And what if he did manage to join forces with the Lakuvi? Not too difficult, Casca reasoned. By now the Lakuvi might be interested in avenging their recent defeat rather than being frightened off by it, as Sonolo and the others so optimistically thought.

He had just had the right amount of whiskey and was sliding drowsily into sleep when Vivita slipped onto the mat beside him. He guessed she'd been tending to the wounded and cleaning up the mess.

He put one arm around her and nuzzled her neck. "Good wife for a chief," he mumbled.

He sat bolt upright. What the fuck was he saying? He didn't want to be chief of this tribe, didn't want to settle down here with Vivita and run this fucking little shanty village. Gotta watch what I'm thinking. He slid back down onto the mat, let his arm fall back around Vivita, and fell asleep.

In the morning Vivita was surprised when he refused to go to the chief's house. He was certain that there was an unavoidable confrontation with Sonolo coming up, and he preferred that Sonolo fuck up as much as possible before he was forced to make his move to take control of the use of the muskets.

Just at that moment Sonolo certainly was fucking up, but in a way that would bring no joy at all to Casca.

When they first landed in Levuka Larsen had gone with Sonolo to the gunsmith, had selected the weapons and negotiated their price. The gunsmith had explained that gunpowder could only be purchased from the government stores and was only supplied on receipt of a written order signed by a suitably respectable person.

"Such as a ship's captain?" And Larsen had made out the order for a keg of powder and given it to Sonolo.

The gunsmith had shown Sonolo how to charge the weapons and had also told him that he must buy the gunpowder from the government store a little farther along the waterfront. But on the way there Sonolo had been distracted by the gaudy prints in another store, and then by the axes and knives, and finally by the whiskey. And the matter of the gunpowder had quite slipped his mind until this moment when he realized that the powder horns were empty.

He sat down in consternation. He had a terrible hangover. Last night he had killed a good friend and a blood relative, and now he was confronted with the fact that he had sold a hundred of his tribesmen into slavery and death for nothing. The shiny new muskets were useless. They would not even make good clubs.

Sonolo got up and walked out of the chief's house. He walked across the square and past his house without stopping, without looking inside where his wife was playing with his youngest son. He walked out of the village and into the jungle.

In the chief's house Semele looked unhappily at the muskets. He did not need to be told that Sonolo had screwed up. He didn't know just what the problem was, but he knew it was a big one. He sat down beside the guns and waited for the problem to show itself.

Within a few minutes the news reached Casca's hut. He didn't understand what it was about, but it seemed that Sonolo had left the village forever and that Semele was left with a big problem with the new guns.

Casca went to the chief's house and saw the old man sitting unhappily beside the muskets. He picked up one, and then the powder horn that lay beside it. Semele saw the same shocked expression on his face that he'd seen on Sonolo's, and he winced as if in pain.

Casca sat down. He had expected a problem, but nothing like this. A hundred of the best men in the village had paid for these guns with their freedom. And they were useless, completely useless. Worse, the village was a hundred young men short for its defense. He looked around, but there was no whiskey in sight.

He looked at Semele. The old man looked deeply wounded, as if something had been taken out of him. He looked up at Casca, waiting to know what he already knew would be the very worst news.

Casca didn't know how to tell him, didn't quite know

how to say it himself. He looked around the village for something he could use as an example—something that needed something else to make it work. Even a canoe without a paddle was far from useless.

He grasped himself by the balls. "Sometimes with a woman, you don't have fire inside for this woman, and nothing happens?"

Semele nodded.

"Is the same with this gun. It needs fire. The fire comes in a powder. No powder, no fire—no fire, gun doesn't work."

Semele nodded again. He didn't understand, but he understood that the guns were useless. It had been his decision to sell men for guns. His decision to sell a hundred men for ten guns rather than ten men for one gun. One useless gun and ten men gone might have been bearable.

Casca searched his mind for some scrap of good news, anything that would go toward alleviating the gloom he could feel growing. It was useless. He felt within himself a despair, a hopelessness that he hadn't felt when he had first faced the necessity to fight Cakabau's guns with wooden clubs.

He shrugged. "Well, we still have clubs."

"Yes," Semele said, "we still have clubs."

"And my .38," Casca added under his breath, "should be great against six muskets."

Semele turned around, and for the first time Casca became aware of the two bodies lying on the ground wrapped in tapa cloth. Obviously one would be Sakuvi. The other, it turned out, was a fine young man, one of the few who did not get drunk on the whiskey, but had stepped between two who did.

The cost of the muskets now stood at a hundred two men. And a few arms, several hands, countless fingers. The axes and knives had taken an enormous toll in the hands of people who had never experienced sharpened steel, and drunk people at that.

Normally, men who had been killed in combat, even this sort of internecine combat, would be eaten, but Semele literally didn't have the stomach for it and ordered that they be buried.

Casca was surprised to see how difficult it was to bury somebody on the island. To bury the bodies in the soft sand on the beach would be pointless—a high tide would uncover them and the whole task would have to be done again. But there was very little clear land, every bit of it was used for farming.

At least a constructive use had been found for the implements that Sonolo had brought from Levuka. The burial party tackled a piece of jungle adjacent to a vegetable patch. They first hacked away all the vines and undergrowth, and then set about felling the several, mainly small trees, and eventually grubbing out the stumps and the roots. It took all the men in the village working for most of the day, but by late afternoon there was a patch of freshly cleared ground and a hole about six feet deep.

The bodies were lowered into the hole on some vines, Mbolo said a few words, a few flowers were thrown in, and the hole was filled.

The people headed home, and it seemed to Casca the two dead men had been virtually forgotten by the time they reached the village.

Certainly they were not the topic of discussion in the chief's house that night. Perhaps that was because there was a more pressing matter to discuss.

When Casca arrived at the chief's house he had already heard something of the matter from Vivita. In fact he had already heard all the details of the sorry story, including the background of Tepole, the one accused of the crime, and about the closest thing to a moral degenerate that the village could boast of.

Tepole came from a respected family and his life had not been significantly different from that of any other young man in the village. Except that from early manhood he had been a nuisance and a menace to everybody, including himself.

Several times in battle he had disgraced himself. He'd stolen personal possessions from other men. And he had a lust for other men's women that repeatedly caused serious trouble, although marital relationships in the village were almost infinitely flexible and two consenting people could do just about whatever they wished. In one of his attempts at unwelcome adultery there had been a fight with the husband, who was killed.

The previous night he had gotten very drunk, but not in the chief's house with everybody else. He'd sneaked away two bottles of whiskey, to get drunk by himself in his hut. Then, this morning, badly hungover, he'd used what was left of the whiskey to get drunk again.

He'd then gone on a lustful rampage through the village, attempting unsuccessfully to get into bed with some of the women who were recovering from wounds received in the melee the night before. By the time he got to the hut of Sala's family, most of the adults in the village were away at the funeral on the mountainside.

He had taken the opportunity to rape Sala, a child of about ten. Her brother Vuki, a year or two younger, had come upon them and attempted to help his sister. In the fracas that followed Tepole had, more or less inadvertently, broken Vuki's neck. He had then tried to strangle Sala and clumsily tried to bury the two bodies in the sand at the top of the beach.

"Teeth of Sirius," Casca muttered, "is there no end to the price of these muskets?"

Sala, recovering while Tepole was digging the grave, escaped. But her brother Vuki was dead.

Tepole's chief accuser was himself. He sat before Semele, but with his back turned, and recited his story of the day's macabre events. Semele interrupted a few times with a searching question, but otherwise all the information came from Tepole of his own accord.

When he had completed his own indictment Semele picked up his great ceremonial war club and paced back and forth behind the seated man, reciting the story of his previous wrongdoings, all of which Tepole agreed with.

Semele then summed up, saying that Tepole was a disgrace, a nuisance and a menace to the village, and that he refused to modify his ways although he'd been given many opportunities.

Semele then pronounced sentence, which was that Tepole was henceforth exiled from the village to the place of refuge, where he must stay until his sins were exonerated. If he were captured before he made it to the place of refuge, or if he should return to the village before it was time, he would be executed.

Casca was incensed. His hut was close to that of Sala's family, and she and her brother Vuki were little rays of sunshine he liked to come across in the village. They were two of the merriest pranksters at spooking Semele unawares. Casca felt that he would gladly strangle Tepole if Semele would allow it.

Tepole immediately left the house, and the kava *bilo* began to pass. Casca inquired about the place of refuge and learned that it was a rock outcrop on the far western edge of the island, all but inaccessible and virtually waterless. If Tepole made it there he would have a very hard, lonely, uncomfortable time.

"But when he returns he will be forgiven?"

"Of course, yes."

"But if he returns too soon, he will be executed?"

"Of course, yes."

"How will he know when it is time?"

"He will know."

Further discussion revealed that Semele's sentence was not quite as lenient as it at first appeared.

Very few exiles made it to the place of refuge without being captured, and the few that did generally returned to the village after only a few days, thus sentencing themselves to death.

This behavior was quite incomprehensible to Casca, who was quite fond of extended periods of his own company, which for the islanders was a condition so extraordinary and intolerable as to make death preferable.

CHAPTER EIGHTEEN

Next morning, he couldn't quite tell why, Casca joined the pursuit party, which consisted of most of the young men in the village.

Vengeance was not a large part of it. Little Sala's death had now fallen into the wider perspective of the hundreds of thousands of deaths in which Casca, one way or another, had been involved. Of itself, the matter of death no longer loomed large in his consciousness or his sensibilities. In fact he envied the dead, so why pretend to mourn or avenge them?

The hunt.

Yes, that was it. Primarily, way back in his psyche, Casca was a hunter. Before he was a warrior he was a hunter. Perhaps he was a warrior because he was a hunter. And of all quarry worth hunting, only man provided what the true hunter really sought—a partner, albeit an unwilling one, in a game where each player is staking his life.

Sure, the odds were unfair, the hunter almost certain to win. But Casca did not play any game for any reason other than to win. If the odds were not in his favor, then unless he had to, he simply didn't play. Those who did wound up cold and lonely in the fields known as cemeteries.

Doomed though he was never to die, he could nonetheless suffer death, and it invariably hurt, and yes, frightened him. He had no wish to do it any more than was absolutely necessary.

Casca did not know how much danger there might be in the hunt after Tepole and he didn't care; it came well inside the odds he was prepared to risk. But as an opponent, even as mere quarry, Tepole sadly disappointed him. Casca seethed with frustration at the man's inadequacies as an adversary.

Although he'd had a clear ten-hour start, Tepole had used hardly any of it, skulking on the edge of the village until just before dawn because he was afraid to venture into the jungle in the dark.

The hunters were even more of a disappointment to Casca. Having found the spot where Tepole had hidden to wait for first light, they returned to the village for a hearty breakfast before setting out in pursuit.

By the time the hunt was joined again, the trail was growing cold and the signs of Tepole's path were getting harder to distinguish. The signs might have been gone altogether had Tepole, in his panic-stricken headlong flight, made an effort to disguise his trail. Casca was disgusted with his lack of enterprise toward the preservation of his own life.

Nor were the hunters at all imaginative in their pursuit. They merely headed in the general direction of the place of refuge, now and again running across some sign of Tepole's passing.

The trail grew progressively colder, and Casca grew more and more bored as he saw that Tepole was easily outdistancing his pursuers. He was tempted to hurry ahead of the hunt and bring down Tepole on his own account. But the chase was so devoid of any real interest for him, and Tepole so easy to track, that he simply couldn't be bothered.

He would have turned around and returned alone to the village, but felt that this might appear somewhat rude. He had made the mistake of joining the hunt, and resolved to stay with it and see just how it ended.

It also occurred to Casca that it might not be a bad idea

for him to know exactly where the refuge was and how to get there quickly. For all he knew, there might yet come a time when he might need such knowledge. More than once he'd seen hospitality turn to hate, and it was far from impossible that he could wind up in the same situation as Tepole.

They came to a narrow neck of land that led out to a broken headland. The trail narrowed until there was barely room for one man to inch his way along, the sheer cliff rearing unclimbable above, the rocks waiting hundreds of feet below.

"How much farther to the refuge?" Casca asked.

"We are in it already," was the reply. "The refuge starts back there where the trail first narrows."

"Then Tepole is home free already?"

"Of course, yes."

But they continued on along the narrow trail, each man risking his life for no sensible reason. The narrow trail came out onto the headland—a rugged, rocky piece of land dotted with small, fruitless trees. A desolate spot.

Tepole had not stopped when he came to the headland, but continued across its width until he was on a projecting spur of rock, with the whole of the refuge between him and his pursuers.

In a far corner of the refuge another man sat. The terrified and confused Tepole did not see or hear or smell him. But even a good hunter like Casca would not have sensed the presence of this man.

Sonolo sat like a figure of stone. Perhaps he heard Tepole—it would have been strange if he did not. But Sonolo had no interest in Tepole or any other mortal man. He had not eaten or tasted water since he left the village; he'd been sitting, as still as an idol, from the moment he arrived at the refuge. His breathing had slowed to a point where it was as imperceptible as the respiration of a stone fish.

He sat staring out to sea, but with his eyes unfocused and unseeing. He was dying, shutting down his body's activities. The process would take many more days, perhaps another week, or even longer.

Tepole sat in the shade of a small tree and looked out to sea. The refuge was at the far western tip of the island, and there was no land to the north or south of the promontory. From where he sat it seemed to Tepole that he could see half of all the world. Even more. When he looked behind him, back toward the world from which he'd been exiled, he saw only the slim, rocky promontory running back to the narrow trail, and beyond it the sea stretched again endlessly to the east around the island. No matter where he looked there was not another person. He was entirely alone.

He leaped to his feet and ran back to the narrow trail. All of the pursuers had by now crossed back out of the refuge and there was no sign of them. A terrible, sickening sensation of loneliness overtook Tepole. Never before in his life had he been alone.

He sat down again, but after a moment was on his feet, pacing restlessly back and forth. He was safe, yes, but what was the good of that? What can a man do alone?

Think.

Tepole sat down, but he could not order his thoughts as he wished. He wanted to think of his wife and of all the other women that he had enjoyed in his life, but it was little Sala who came to his mind, and her brother Vuki, whom he had killed. When he did succeed in pushing these two from his mind, he found himself thinking of Lascoa, whom he'd killed when Lascoa had caught him trying to rape his wife. These thoughts were replaced by memories of his cowardice in battle. He couldn't manage to think of anything from his past life that afforded him any satisfaction.

And here there was nothing to think about—no women, not even any man. Nothing that might amuse him. True, he should be thinking about food, but he was too much in turmoil to be hungry, much less think about finding something to eat.

He sat and stared at the blue void before him. The featureless sea ran flat in every direction. There was no horizon. At some point that couldn't be distinguished the blue sea merged with the clear blue sky.

"*Moana,*" Tepole muttered. The word included both the sea and sky, all that he could see to the west. He turned to look back to the east. There was only the towering cliff, girt by the endless *moana* to the south, and if he were to walk but a few hundred paces north he would see again the endless *moana* extending to the eastern horizon.

The only land in all the world, it seemed, was the small space of the refuge. To find anything more, any sign of his own kind, he must go back across the narrow trail by the cliff. And that meant death.

Nonetheless Tepole found himself constantly drawn back to this trail. Once he thought he heard a faint sound, like a voice carried to him on the wind. But his ears were not adept at distinguishing sounds. There were no animals on the island, and Tepole had never acquired any of the attributes of a hunter.

Perhaps it had been a bird. Nearby he heard a small bird and saw its movement in a tree.

But he lingered and listened, heard more sounds like the movements of men, and crept out a little onto the narrow neck of the trail to listen more.

A better hunter might have seen Casca lying, thoroughly bored, just beyond where the trail opened out into a broader space.

As far as Casca could tell the whole morning's effort had been pointless. They had never really tried to catch Tepole or head him off from the refuge. He had outdistanced them without any real effort and was now safe in the refuge. Why then, Casca wondered, did they still linger, sprawled about in the shade in the broad, clear space just before the cliff and the trail that led into the refuge? Only politeness and a sense of consideration for his hosts' ways of doing things prevented Casca from leaving the clearing to return to the village.

He rolled over on the ground to look at the entrance to the refuge, and as he did so he thought he saw something moving. He concentrated his gaze and made out the shape of a man, undoubtedly Tepole, crouching amongst some bushes just at the edge of the clearing.

Was the man mad? Tepole was already back outside the refuge and therefore a legitimate target for anybody in the pursuit party. Casca could easily shoot him from where he lay. Perhaps one of the others could hit him with a well-thrown rock. Maybe one of them could creep close enough to tackle him.

But none of the others gave any sign that they had seen Tepole, and Casca guessed they were unaware of their quarry only a few yards away.

Then Tepole moved, the sounds unmistakable, his movement revealing him clearly among the bushes. Still nobody gave any sign of awareness of his presence.

Casca watched as Tepole crept closer and closer, coming farther and farther from his only place of safety. He stumbled clumsily and almost fell, making a great deal of noise, at last alerting the others to his presence.

Dukuni, the fisherman chief, who seemed to me more or less in charge of the hunt, laughed and flung a stone in the fugitive's general direction. Tepole sprang up into full view and ran for the refuge.

Casca chuckled. "I'll bet he doesn't stop till he gets to the far side of the refuge," he said to himself.

He would have been surprised, even astonished, had he seen Tepole come to a stop a few paces along the cliff trail.

Dukuni got to his feet and the others did likewise. They left the clearing and headed back toward the village. Casca was pleased. The boring business of the pursuit of the condemned man seemed to be over.

But at the next clearing everybody stopped again. There were bananas and papayas growing, and Casca picked some fruit and lay on the ground to eat it.

He heard Tepole before he saw him. The fool had come almost into the clearing, trying, it seemed, to get close enough to the men to hear the scattered snatches of idle conversation.

Casca watched Tepole as he came closer and closer. He moved clumsily, waving branches and bushes, betraying his position long before Casca could see him clearly. The man's lack of jungle craft amazed Casca, who had grown up in the streets of the city of Rome and had already been a battle-scarred veteran when he first saw jungle.

He'd learned about it damned fast in order to stay alive. But in this jungle there were no ferocious cats, hyenas, snakes, pythons, or alligators. Nor was there any game to be hunted, so Tepole had never learned to hunt or to hide in the jungle.

As he had got closer he made more and more noise, and finally aroused the attention of Dukuni and his men.

"I should shoot the dumb bastard now," Casca muttered, "but I don't want to show this gun. The fool will probably follow us all the way to the village anyway."

He probably would have, but Dukuni had other ideas. Perhaps he, too, had become bored with the game. He gave a signal and the warriors stood up. Casca realized that less than half the men had come into the glade.

The warriors began to move slowly toward where Tepole was hiding, and he got up and ran. After only a few steps he let out a yelp and stopped. His way was blocked by another line of warriors, who had stayed behind along the trail.

Tepole turned and ran a few useless steps toward where Dukuni waited, spun around to run away once more but again stopped short of the line of warriors. For a few moments he hesitated, shuffling a step or two toward one party of his pursuers then back toward the others.

At last he gave up and sank to the ground.

All the warriors squatted where they were. After a few moments Tepole stood up and started to walk, heading back toward the village.

Nobody spoke to him or obstructed his way or acknowledged his existence. Tepole walked at his own pace and they simply accompanied him, spread out behind him in a half circle cutting off any possibility of retreat to the refuge.

When they arrived back at the village nobody acknowledged his presence either. Tepole did not go to his hut, and his wife and children did not come out to see him. He moved about the village like a lost soul, speaking to nobody; the people, even the small children, behaving as if he were not there.

Casca noticed that Dukuni now carried a club, but he made no move toward Tepole, who seemed to be free to wander the village as he wished, drifting aimlessly here and there, making no effort at communication. He moved about like a sleepwalker.

Suddenly it was over.

Casca happened to be looking in Tepole's direction at the time, but he hardly knew what happened. Tepole was lying on the ground, blood pouring from his ears, and Dukuni, his great war club on his shoulder, was walking away.

Half a dozen warriors picked up the body and carried it out of the village, a score or so more following. Casca followed too.

They headed west again, and Casca guessed they were carrying the corpse back to the place of refuge.

Along the way they changed porters several times, but without stopping, so that they came to the refuge a little before sunset.

At the narrow neck of the trail leading into the refuge, one of the warriors slung the body over his left shoulder and moved quickly along the path, leaning into the cliff face as the weight tended to pull him away from it.

Casca shook his head in amazement. "The fucker's dead or dying anyway, why not drop him in the sea?" he muttered.

The warrior negotiated the dangerous trail and at the other end handed the body over to four others, who carried it all the way across the small sanctuary and threw it onto a pile of bones where a point ran out over the sea.

Nobody took any further interest, and they began to leave the refuge. Casca lingered to look down the cliff.

At the bottom there was a large, flat expanse of rock jutting out into the ocean with a small patch of calm water on its lee side. Casca saw that it would be just possible to climb down the cliff to this area of flat rock.

CHAPTER NINETEEN

As the *bilo* passed in the chief's house that night the conversations were all about Sakuvi, his life, his achievements, and his amiability, and about the little boy, Vuki, the fun he had enjoyed in his short life and his stout defense of his sister.

Casca listened attentively to all the conversations but could not pick up any reference to Tepole, the days hunt, his death, or the disposal of his corpse. He had expected the usual ritual of repeated recital of all the events of the day until every detail was know by everybody.

But it seemed that this was not a day to be remembered. Nor was Tepole to be remembered, neither his crimes nor his punishment.

Sakuvi and Vuki and the departed Sonolo, on the other hand, were talked of at great length, and songs grew out of the conversations that recorded their lives and their deaths, carrying the moral that whiskey had brought about the end of all three.

But Vuki's murderer was not mentioned by name. It was as if Tepole had never existed.

And, too, it was as if Cakabau didn't exist. Casca strove with all the language he could muster, and with remarks in English to Semele and Mbolo, to make the threatened raid the topic of conversation, but without success. So far the attack had not happened, perhaps it never would.

The villagers were heartily sick of the topic. Already the threatened raid had cost them their hundred best men, the whiskey casualties, and Sala's brother. Tepole was not counted as a loss.

Frustrated, Casca withdrew from the conversation and sat back to relax and enjoy the kava, and later Vivita, or which other woman wound up in his bed for the night.

He looked around at the likely contenders. There were half a dozen young women, all, at the moment, staying respectfully a little farther from him than Vivita. But Casca now knew that this might change in the course of the evening, that the game amongst the women never stopped. Through some process of communication, competition, and cooperation that he'd not been able to discern much less appreciate or understand, Casca was aware that the women might decide amongst themselves that he should spend the night with one of these young lovelies rather than with the gap-toothed Vivita.

The kava was beginning to take hold. Casca felt the pleasant, numbing sensation spreading throughout his body, felt the tension and worry about Cakabau's raid seeping away. The soft light from the fire and the whale-oil lamps was becoming a golden glow.

The little blue stones around Takuni's neck reflected the soft light very pleasantly. Casca watched the firelight glinting off the facets of the stones and wondered what they were. Surely not cut, he decided they must be some naturally occurring crystal.

Suddenly he was on his feet, snatching at the little necklace, holding the stones in the palm of his hand and studying them intently.

"Where do these come from?" he demanded.

Takuni was taken aback. So was everybody else. It seemed that Casca was forgetting his manners.

Takuni shrugged uncomfortably. "From the mountain. There are many, if you search for them."

"And yellow?" Casca shouted. "Are there yellow ones too?"

"Of course, yes." Takuni shrugged again. "But the yellow stuff crumbles in your fingers. These are much prettier."

Casca whooped like a delighted schoolboy. He threw his clenched fists into the air as if to throw them away and stamped his feet and grunted and shouted. He grabbed Takuni by the waist and lifted her high above his head.

Semele, Mbolo, Ateca, Duana, and even the imperturbable Vivita stared at him in amazement.

He put down the girl, raced across to Semele, and lifted the astonished giant in his arms. He put him down and whirled about to do the same to Mbolo.

"Gunpowder!" he shouted. "Gunpowder! Great balls of Mars, we've got gunpowder!"

Semele looked up from where Casca had dropped him. A lesser man might have suffered a considerable loss of dignity.

"What is gunpowder?" he asked politely.

Casca whooped some more, shouted, "Gunpowder, gunpowder, gunpowder," stamped his feet, waved his fists, danced a sort of barbaric jig, and finally collapsed to the floor laughing.

Semele, Mbolo, and the others waited patiently and politely for his outburst to pass.

Lying on the floor, Casca made the gesture of an erection with his right arm and clenched fist. "Force," he shouted. He clutched his balls in his left hand and opened the right fist explosively. "Fire," he yelled. "Life for the muskets."

When at last his hilarity diminished, Casca sputtered an explanation through his chuckles. "We can use the muskets. The men have not been wasted. Sonolo's mission will yet defeat Cakabau and save the village."

In the morning Casca awoke to a breakfast of papayas and cooked bananas and coconut milk, prepared by Takuni. He held out his hand and she dropped the necklace into it. He grunted happily as the sight of the crystals confirmed his idea of the previous night.

"You can find some more of these stones for me now?"

"Of course, yes."

"And the soft yellow stuff?"

"Of course, yes."

"Good, let's go."

He gulped a mouthful of coconut milk, snatched up some bananas, and left the hut at such a pace that Takuni had to run to catch up with him.

"We shall need a bag," she gasped.

"Get one," Casca snapped, and kept right on heading for the lower slopes of the volcano.

Takuni ran to her hut and returned with a tapa sack, trotting to keep up with Casca, who was striding along at the phenomenal speed that he had first learned in Caesar's legions, covering a full six feet every time his left foot hit the ground.

They struck directly up the face of the mountain, ignoring the curving trail until the going got so steep that they had to use it.

His pace didn't slacken. He climbed like a man possessed. After the several days of frustration and inaction he now saw the opportunity to do something, and luxuriated in the sweat streaming from every pore of his body.

His little companion managed to keep up with him, but in some confusion. To move so fast under the broiling tropical sun was an absurdity to her. Did this blue-eyed madman fear that the mountain would go away?

After some hours of climbing at Casca's frenetic pace they came at last to the lip of the volcanic crater. Casca stood on the edge and looked down across the expanse of black lava. Huge waves of molten rock racing from the core had hardened in place when the fires cooled, and they now formed a great, black, frozen sea.

They climbed down into the crater and made their way across the lava, sometimes having to climb the arching face of a wave six to eight feet tall. Then the waves were smaller, only ripples, and then the frozen puddle of lava was flat.

It was hot underfoot, and from time to time the surface crust broke away and they fell through the trapped bubbles of air, sometimes only an inch, but often a foot or more. Casca's heart was in his mouth at the thought that they might be crashing right through the surface lava and down into the fires beneath.

They came to the crumbling inner edge of the crater and looked down. Far below them red fires glowed and sulfurous fumes drifted up to them.

"The very halls of Hades," Casca muttered. "Where do we find the stones?" he asked Takuni.

"Everywhere," she said, and smiled, "and nowhere. It is necessary to search."

"Yeah," grunted Casca, "well, there's hours of light left, let's get to it." He moved to skirt the fire pit. "You go that way, and yell out if you see anything—blue or yellow."

The sun burned down out of the clear blue sky. The lava underfoot was almost too hot to touch. Casca cursed that he had not brought some water. He seemed to be moving in small clouds of steam issuing in puffs from the hot ground.

He plodded about on the hot, black stone, bored now with the tiresome task of searching for tiny flecks of color in the endless sea of black.

Across the pit Takuni was capering about like a child at a picnic, darting first in one direction where she thought she saw some color, then disappointed, swerving away to run a few paces another way.

Her scatterbrained mode of searching half annoyed, but also amused Casca, who was diligently quartering the area, carefully examining every tiny cleft and crevice. He was about to call to Takuni to search more carefully when she gave a shriek of unmistakable delight and Casca found himself bounding eagerly to her side.

She had come to where the ripples of lava rose again into waves, and was looking up the back of a long rise of black dotted with tiny flecks of yellow.

Casca sucked in his breath in disappointment. It would take hours to dig out just one ounce of these tiny little dots of sulfur.

Takuni was running up the back of the wave, to jump off its crest and race to the next one.

Casca shrugged and took out his knife. "Well," he muttered, "maybe she'll find some bluestone while I'm winkling out this stuff."

But another delighted yelp from Takuni had him bounding up the back of the wave and leaping from its face as she had. In the back of the next wave he could see a broad swathe of yellow where the lightweight sulfur had frothed to the top of the denser lava.

Casca fell upon the vein of yellow and dug out great chunks of it, catching them in his left hand and gesturing to Takuni to bring him the tapa sack.

Takuni did so, first taking out the two coconuts she had carried with her from the village. Casca looked at the little black girl in amazement.

"What else did you think of that I forgot?" he asked as he opened a coconut and gulped thirstily from it.

For an answer Takuni reached into the sack and brought out a small green-stone axe.

Casca sheathed his knife and held out his hand. As Takuni handed him the axe he took both her hands in his and kissed her gently on the lips.

She responded willingly. Casca looked around. In the entire expanse of the crater there was no grass, not even a patch of bare soil, nothing but the hard, black, hot rock with its broken, crumbling edges. To lay the girl down on the sharp rock was unthinkable; it would lacerate her back to strips.

"I'd cut my knees to bits too," Casca grunted, handing Takuni the coconut and going to work with the axe. "This is enough of the yellow stuff. Look for the bluestones." He turned all his attention to his digging.

For a moment Takuni stood looking at him as if disappointed, then she scaled the wave of lava, jumped off the edge, and ran skipping for the next rearing black wall.

Casca wielded the little axe with a will, chopping away the brittle rock and scooping out handfuls of the soft yellow sulfur. He was coming to the end of the vein when he heard Takuni calling from a long way away.

He clambered up to stand erect on the crust of lava, six feet or so above the general flow. He could see Takuni waving from a great distance, almost to the far side of the crater.

Hurriedly he scooped all the free sulfur into the sack and set off at a half run, whooping exultantly as he went.

When he got to Takuni she was down on her hands and knees, peering down into a tiny crevice in the rock.

She moved aside to let him see.

Tiny wisps of sulfurous steam issued from deep down in the crevice and condensed onto its walls on the way to the surface. The steam carried with it tiny traces of copper and sulfur that had been chemically welded together in the giant caldron below. Here and there on the sides of the crevice the condensed steam had deposited tiny blue crystals of copper sulfate.

Casca seized Takuni and kissed her rapturously. She hugged him fiercely.

"What the hell," Casca muttered, "this old hide can stand a few more scars." He lowered himself to the ground, and she was quickly astride him. He didn't even notice the way the broken edge of the rock sawed his back to a bloody mess.

It was dark before they got out of the crater, but Casca was well satisfied with the day's prospecting. He had perhaps twenty or so ounces of pure sulfur and about the same weight of copper sulfate. He had also collected several long sticks of obsidian, the volcanic glasslike stone that formed in the intense heat of the fiery magma.

They made their way down the mountain and back to the village, going directly to Takuni's house, where she quickly prepared a meal of cassava, taro, breadfruit, and bananas. Then they lay down together on the sleeping mat.

It was mid morning when Casca awoke. He had slept through the morning drums and all the hubbub of Takuni's household as they awoke, washed, breakfasted, and left the house to attend to the day's work.

Casca and Takuni were alone in the house, and she brought him a breakfast of small fish in coconut cream as soon as she saw that he was awake. When he'd eaten she walked with him to his own hut, turning aside to go her own way when they were almost there.

He set to work at once, pounding up the small blue crystals, sieving the sulfur through tapa cloth, and finally combining the two with some of the saltpeter that Larsen had left for pickling fish and some charcoal from Vivita's cook fire.

Casca's homemade explosive worked as well as he could have wished. His first test resulted in wild shrieks of terror from all over the village, a general flight from the vicinity, and a great deal of confusion.

But soon curiosity overcame fear, and for his next test he had an audience of the entire daytime population of the village. Casca added some torn strips of cloth to the mix, bundled the whole in banana leaves between two *bilos* wrapped in sharkskin and tied tightly with vines, and launched it, using for mortar a clay pot wrapped around many times in sharkskin.

The pot disintegrated in all directions as the first charge exploded, but contained the blast long enough to hurl the *bilos* aloft, where they burst apart mightily as their charge detonated. The air was filled with blue smoke and prettily fluttering strips of cloth. The show was a huge success with the villagers, and Casca himself was mightily pleased.

"Fuck Cakabau," he shouted, "we'll blow the bastard's balls off."

His hundreds of years of rigorous self-discipline, frequent lapses into comfortable daydreams, and a drastic awareness of the seemingly inevitable results of such lapses put a stop to his celebratory mood.

"Of course, if he strikes at dawn tomorrow, we'll be as defenseless as we were a week ago."

There was no time to be lost. Ten musketeers had to be selected and trained tonight. Now.

Casca went looking for the carpenter chief. He needed a lot of help before tonight's meeting. He found Watolo making a stone-headed club, and explained to him what he needed while he watched him work.

Watolo had heated a stone over a slow fire of coconut shells, and using a length of split bamboo as a tongs, he now removed it from the fire and carefully dripped water on it, one drop at a time, chips of stone flying off. When the stone became too cool for his chipping to take place, he reheated it and repeated the process until he had formed a hole through its center. Forcing a tapered stick through the hole, he then hammered it on a large, hard rock until it was roughly rounded. Twirling the stick in his hands, he worked a saucer-shaped dent in the rock till it was smooth.

He fitted a new tapered handle of the tough, hard, black root used for wooden clubs, with a few inches of the fat end protruding through the stone like the handle of a mattock. He fixed the handle in place with gum from the breadfruit tree. In use, centrifugal force would progressively tighten the head further onto the handle.

CHAPTER TWENTY

In the chief's house Casca had no difficulty in getting the villagers' attention. The afternoon's demonstration had seen to that. But Casca was worried that tonight's demonstration might move the villagers to such transports of optimism that he would be unable to get the necessary urgency behind the training of the musketeers.

So he opened the night's demonstration by taking one of the muskets, priming it with his homemade powder, ramming home a ball, the wad, and then shooting Semele's ceremonial war club into splinters.

The clamor to be allowed to use the weapon was immense, and Semele's amused amazement ensured that he be the first to try.

Mbolo was next, then his son, and finally Ateca, thinking that perhaps a woman's touch was needed. But none of them succeeded in putting even a scratch on the club they were shooting at.

Casca took a considerably longer time to load the next musket, meanwhile calling upon all the watchers to observe how much of the precious gunpowder was consumed.

He then blew to bits a second club, and pointed out that some training was needed, and called for competitors in a contest to select the ten musketeers.

Every man and most of the women demanded to be allowed to compete, which suited Casca fine. If he could teach the whole village at once, so much the better.

Casca firmly believed that there is nothing quite so useless as an unloaded gun, and also maintained that even in the hands of an untrained idiot a loaded gun will at least make a frightening noise, so he first set to work to teach everybody how to load the weapons.

Demonstrating with one musket, he quickly showed ten people how to pour in the powder, place the ball, ram home the wad, and set the cap. Within a few minutes each of the ten was giving a close demonstration to a dozen or so others, then more were trying and being corrected by Casca. Pretty soon everybody in the house knew what the loading operation looked like, and quite a number had tried it.

Next Casca took away all the powder and shot and showed ten men how to aim their guns at the men of coconut palm and bamboo that Watolo had made for him earlier in the evening. Each man target had a large hole where the navel might have been, and the contenders were told to aim at this point. By crouching behind the target and sighting through this hole, Casca could tell which men might have some chance of keeping a musket trained on a man.

An agreeably large number qualified on this rough test, and Casca soon had ten of them slowly squeezing off practice shots with the promise that whoever impressed him as being gentlest, slowest, and smoothest on the trigger would get to fire a live charge.

As the finale of the evening Dukuni's son Lobo was awarded the privilege of actually firing at the target.

To Casca's immense satisfaction he punched a hole through the target's belly just alongside the target hole. He was especially delighted at Lobo's lament that he had not succeeded in placing the ball exactly through the hole.

By the time he and Vivita walked to their hut, Casca felt confident that the village was capable of giving Cakabau a very bad shock should he appear in the morning.

But to Casca's delight Cakabau did not appear in the

morning. Every day counted, and that day Casca made determined use of every minute that passed.

He now had all of Sonolo's authority as war chief, and Semele and Mbolo willingly added all of theirs, but it was the novelty of playing with the muskets that provided him with the main incentive for the warriors to undergo his prescribed training.

He had selected an elite group of thirty warriors, all, he judged, likely to prove competent shots, and swift, sure loaders. He kept them practicing all day, loading the muskets with fine sand, balls, and undersized wads, then unloading them and repeating the process over and over.

From what Kini had told him, it was clear that Cakabau's men were less than competent with their weapons, and especially slow and clumsy at reloading. By using his weapons in relays and reloading quickly, Casca hoped to maximize the effectiveness of the ten guns to the point where Cakabau, and perhaps even Savage—if the white man accompanied his slave raiders—would believe themselves hopelessly outgunned, giving the villagers a big psychological advantage.

If the psychology didn't work, then speedy reloading and accurate fire would be all the more urgent.

By way of relief, and as reward, the fastest loaders were allowed to play at shooting at the targets, one man crouching behind to sight through the hole and shouting when the shooter's musket lined up exactly on his eye.

There was not enough power for practice firing, but from time to time Casca would reward especially good work by allowing a live shot at the target. He manipulated this reward to ensure that each of the thirty men got to fire at least one shot.

Casca was delighted with his musketeers, and was also more than pleased with his two club-wielding squads of about the same size. With the assistance of Semele and Mbolo he had modified some of the movements of the traditional war dances so that, on command, the warriors could speedily execute some maneuvers that were new to them, and he hoped would be devastatingly novel to Cakabau's men.

That night he persuaded Semele to bring the kava drinking to an early close, and he went to bed with Vivita, hoping earnestly that Cakabau would attack in the morning.

CHAPTER TWENTY-ONE

Casca was not disappointed.

The wooden drums roused him just before dawn, as usual, but sounded again while he was enjoying a leisurely breakfast.

The village fishermen, hanging off the reef for the early morning catch, had spotted six great war canoes approaching from the eastern end of the island, and had raced for the shore to give the alarm.

"They come then from the Lakuvi village. We can expect the Lakuvi men to attack us, too, from the land side."

"Damn," Casca muttered, annoyed. He should have posted lookouts on the mountaintop to watch for Savage's schooner sneaking into anchorage on the northern side of the island. Well, it was all right. So they must also face the Lakuvi and their clubs, but at least Savage had not sailed into the lagoon with his cannon.

Almost the entire population of the village ran to the beach to wait for the invaders, dancing, shouting, waving war clubs.

The fishermen deployed themselves about the lagoon in another show of strength, hurling abuse and insults and small rocks at the enemy canoes as they came through the opening of the reef. But whenever one of Cakabau's men put down his paddle to reach for a musket, the fishermen

143

would retreat, dodging across the water so that the enemy warrior could not get a clean, close shot.

By the time canoes reached the beach all six of the enemy muskets had been discharged, but none of the Navola fishermen had been hit.

For a moment Casca contemplated a pitched battle on the beach before the enemy could reload. But his own muskets were in the village, a fight with clubs might be inconclusive, and a defeat would be disastrous.

As the men from Bau got out of their canoes to push them ashore they were assailed from all sides with a hail of flying stones. The small missiles, thrown from a great distance, did no real harm, but served to irritate the attackers and to let them know that they could expect a fight.

Casca was relieved to see that there were only the six muskets, and he was delighted to see how slowly and carelessly they were rereadied for firing.

At a signal from Casca everybody withdrew from the beach, and the fishermen ran their boats ashore as far away as possible from the attackers. Before the last of the enemy had waded ashore, the villagers were safely behind the palisade.

All, that is, except Vivita and five of the prettiest women in the village, who hid themselves in the jungle fringe near where the enemy canoes were drawn up on the beach.

The women waited until the enemy started toward the village then moved toward the three warriors standing guard over the canoes. When they were close to the canoes Vivita, Takuni, and Luisa stepped out of the jungle and approached the guards.

The women stopped a few yards away, as if only now realizing that these were the enemy. The guards looked at them, looked at each other, and looked carefully around at the space between the beach and the village, where there was nothing to be seen but the backs of their own men.

Nonalau grinned to his companions. "They know we get them later, anyway, so they come to give themselves first. Good."

"Very good. Very good," the others agreed.

Nonalau held out his hand in a gesture of friendship, and Vivita responded, slowly moving toward him one step at a time.

When she was only a few paces from his canoe, Nonalau ran for her, the other two warriors running for her companions. The women shrieked playfully and ran away, allowing themselves to be caught after only a few paces.

As the enemy warriors bore them to the ground the other three women slipped from the jungle and ran to hide in the water behind the sterns of the canoes. They went to work on the hulls with augers of obsidian stone.

The sticks of volcanic glass had been chipped to broad, sharp points, and as each girl turned the stone in her hands the sharp edges bit into the wood, drilling a neat hole below the waterline.

The guards had lost all interest in the canoes and in their own warriors, who were advancing on the village.

Casca had made Lobo his deputy, and he dispatched him with thirty clubs to meet the attackers halfway down the slope to the beach.

Cakabau's men were advancing in no particular order, and reacted with some surprise to see the village warriors blocking their path.

The biggest and most powerfully built of the enemy warriors was at their head, carrying a musket, and Casca assumed that this was the mighty Cakabau himself. He brought up his musket and fired at the village defenders.

But as he raised the weapon, Lobo gave a warning shout and the Navola men threw themselves to the ground, as Casca had trained them to do.

The ball fell harmlessly short.

"Trigger happy," chuckled Casca behind the palisade. "Good. Very good."

The enemy vanguard was now closer, another warrior stopping to level his musket.

Again the defenders flattened themselves, and this time the ball passed harmlessly over their heads.

Casca signaled the drummers to beat the retreat, and the

defenders scrambled to their feet and ran back toward the village.

Cakabau stopped to reload his musket, and his warriors gathered around him. It was clear from the tone of their shouted conversation that this battle was already going disturbingly differently from any of their previous raids. An enemy who knew how to avoid the power of their deadly fire sticks was something entirely new to them.

Casca's drummers sounded a halt to the retirement and the warriors made another stand, clubs at shoulder as if determined to come directly to blows with the attackers.

Cakabau barked an order, and all six of his musketeers raised their weapons.

Immediately, in another of Casca's rehearsed maneuvers, the line of defenders fell apart, warriors running wildly in all directions away from the guns.

Moving targets were outside the experience of these shooters, and they tried to aim their guns first this way, then that way, and all six shots went harmlessly wild.

There was a great outburst of confused shouting, and for a moment Casca toyed again with the thought of a sudden attack while the guns were unloaded. But the day was very young. There was plenty of time for the undoing of the great cannibal king, and the longer it took, the more thoroughly he might be undone.

Casca had carefully thought through the whole battle plan and intended day-long harrassment of the enemy under the hot sun while most of his own troops rested in the shade and ate at their leisure, relaxing until the cool of the late afternoon, when the real battle would commence.

When the muskets were reloaded Casca's drummers again sounded the retreat, and this time the defenders retired behind the palisade before any shots were fired.

Cakabau's men pursued them, stopping about a hundred paces from the fence, where they formed up in three formidable-looking ranks, all but the six musketeers in the center hefting war clubs—a hundred twenty of the biggest, healthiest warriors Casca had ever seen. They began a fierce, challenging war dance.

At once, and before Casca had time to speak, about half the village defenders leaped over the palisade and took up an opposing position, dancing, shouting, gesturing.

Casca shouted to the drummers for the retreat, but had to repeat the order several times before they responded.

Then the sound of the drums was lost in the crashing explosions of the six muskets and two men were lying dead on the field and another was flapping about in agony like a wounded bird, a shattered arm hanging useless from one shoulder.

The rest of the men made it back inside the palisade where Casca was tearing his hair in frustration.

Next to him Semele groaned, "We have lost."

"Like fuck we have," Casca shouted. "The battle hasn't even started."

"The battle is over," Semele wailed. "We have lost two men."

Looking at the chief, Casca realized that he had indeed already surrendered. He drew his .38, clapped it to the head of the nearest man and blew out his brains.

There was one great communal shriek, then silence. Casca pointed his little revolver at the man with the wounded arm and shot him through the heart, then turned the gun on Semele.

"This weapon needs no reloading," he lied. "One more word of surrender and I will kill you."

He turned the weapon on Mbolo and then Ateca. "I will kill you and Mbolo and Ateca, and everybody in the village before Cakabau reaches the outer wall."

Semele and Mbolo looked at each other. Ateca and Duana shook their heads. Semele closed his eyes for a moment, then looked at Casca.

"What do you wish for us to do?"

"Fight, you bastards, fight. We're going to win this day. We're going to drive Cakabau from this island forever."

As if to answer this boast there was a great beating of war drums in the near distance, and a hundred or so Lakuvi warriors burst into the clearing, war clubs at the ready.

"Shit," muttered Casca, "just what I need."

He grabbed Lobo by the arm. "That's the end of our harrassment plan. We've got to fight now. Get the men back outside."

Lobo nodded vigorously and started yelling at his warriors.

They formed up inside the palisade, as they had rehearsed all the previous day. They were puzzled, worried, and not a little afraid, but when Lobo shouted the order they leaped over the wall to take up positions only a dozen or so paces from the attackers. They executed a brief war dance and suddenly charged.

Cakabau and his men were astonished to see less than a quarter of their own number charging at them, but quickly prepared to repulse the attack. Those with the muskets ran to the rear to get out of the fight while they reloaded.

The front ranks of the two armies met in a great clash of wooden clubs. Cakabau's superior numbers milled around, trying to get at the much smaller group of defenders.

At a shout from Lobo the whole front row of defenders dropped to the ground as if felled by the enemy's clubs.

The astonished attackers found themselves looking into the muzzles of ten muskets. And a second later five of the muskets roared and five of the attackers fell, clutching their bellies.

At the same instant another squad of the thirty men came leaping over the wall, and then another.

The men from Lakuvi were still racing toward the scene, under the impression that the musket fire came only from the ranks of their allies, the men from Bau.

The Navola men who had dropped to the ground scrambled back to their feet, laying about their clubs. The five defenders with real muskets turned and ran back to the palisade to hurl their guns over the wall and snatch the clubs that were handed to them to race back into the battle.

The two new squads had run to the flanks of the attacking force, and Cakabau's force divided to meet the assaults that were now coming from three different directions.

Cakabau and his other musketeers came rushing from

the rear, but ran into the solid wall of the backs of their own men.

While Cakabau was trying to reorganize his men, the confronting squad of Navola men suddenly broke off the action, turning to run back to the palisade.

Cakabau had just succeeded in restraining his front row in order to bring his muskets into action, and now their targets were fleeing to safety. He swung his own musket on the squad to his left, shouting to the others to fire too.

His men were still adjusting their aim when the front ranks of both Navola squads dropped to the ground, revealing what looked like twenty muskets. Five of these muskets fired and three Bau men fell mortally wounded.

Casca appeared in the small opening in the palisade, where he set up three mortars tilted up just slightly from the horizontal. One after another the charges exploded, hurling their missiles amongst the enemy ranks, where they in turn exploded, spattering almost every man with small stones and seashells. This small shrapnel did little real harm, but completely demoralized the attackers.

At the same instant ten more men, armed with what looked like muskets, leaped over the wall, followed by Casca, a war club in his left hand and the .38 in his right.

The men from Lakuvi were now close enough to see this white warrior who had already defeated them once. They were also close enough to see that Cakabau was getting very much the worse of it and that the defending villagers seemed to have many, many more muskets than the attackers.

They turned and ran back the way they had come, throwing away their clubs as they raced for the safety of their own village.

Casca called his men to a halt, the muskets were leveled, the five real ones belched flame, and five more of the attackers lay writhing on the ground.

Cakabau's men broke and ran for the beach, three more falling in the new crossfire from the defenders' reloaded muskets. Followed by his men, Cakabau raced for the beach and the canoes that would carry them to safety.

On the beach the three guards were trying to disentangle themselves from the arms and legs of the women as they realized that something had gone very wrong.

In panting passion the women clung to them, the men trying to get free, yet still thrusting into the hot, writhing bodies of the women.

As each man did succeed in freeing himself, his woman scrambled away, hurling handfuls of sand at the men as they ran for their lives.

Halfway down the slope to the beach Casca called for his gunners to stop and reload while the rest raced screaming and shouting after the retreating warriors, who were abandoning not only their clubs, but also the now useless muskets, powder horns, and bags of shot and wad. Only Cakabau kept his weapon, but made no attempt to stop and reload it.

The raiders gained the beach and pushed their canoes into the water, leaping into them and driving them through the shallows with expert and powerful strokes.

In a few yards the canoes were half full of water, the bailers useless against the streams pouring into each boat through a dozen different holes. Another few yards and the boats were under the water, the men still doggedly paddling, but the heavy canoes scarcely moving.

Several men jumped out of the canoes and attempted to lift them in the water while others bailed frantically. But it was hopeless. In a few minutes it was clear that the canoes had been rendered useless, and the men abandoned them to swim for the shore.

In the shallows the men of Navola waited, war clubs and muskets at the ready. Casca restrained the musketeers, but the clubs made short work of the few enemy who reached the shore.

The others swam farther along the lagoon, but the defenders kept pace with them on the beach, and wherever the enemy stumbled ashore exhausted, there were clubs waiting for them.

Casca stood a moment in indecision. Riding at anchor on the other side of the island was Savage's schooner, which represented perhaps Casca's only real hope of escape from the island. He could take a hundred men and paddle around the island to Savage's ship to reach it around dusk, when they would surely be taken for Cakabau's men returning in victory. With the captured muskets, powder, and shot, they could surely take the ship, and the demoralized Lakuvi men most likely would not fight.

Savage he would execute out of hand, together with his officers, and if necessary all of the crew. But it was likely that most of them would choose service under Casca in preference to instant death. He would not only be able to leave the island, but would be well equipped to make a slaving raid on some nearby island.

The plan started falling apart. Casca realized that Savage recruited his slaves with the full knowledge and cooperation of the British authorities in Levuka, so Casca would not be able to take his stolen ship there. Nor, he knew, could he land slaves in Australia unless they had been properly indentured in a British colony.

"Aw, fuck it," he muttered, looking around to see that his troops were now totally out of control and that not even the threat of his .38 would serve to get a hundred of them into the canoes.

There were a dozen or so warriors, and Cakabau himself still alive and swimming when Semele suggested to Casca that they be allowed to escape.

"To carry the tale," the old chief said.

Casca agreed, and he, Lobo, Semele, and Mbolo eventually managed to restrain their warriors. By the time the last enthusiastic club stroke landed there were six survivors and the cannibal king swimming desperately for the far eastern end of the lagoon.

Casca signaled to the men holding the loaded muskets. There was a great roar of explosive, and three of the swimmers died in the water.

Semele looked around him. There were dead bodies all the way along the beach.

"How can we eat so many?" he asked in dismay.

Duana looked at him shrewdly. "Perhaps the Lakuvi would help us."

Semele nodded. "Perhaps they would."

He called two warriors to him and told him to run to the Lakuvi village and invite the entire village to the feast.

The banquet started as soon as they returned to the village.

Casca munched his way unconcernedly through a set of genitals, a liver, a heart, and some kidneys before starting on a buttock steak.

Everybody in the village had enjoyed some of the meat by the time the Lakuvi villagers arrived, and they pressed various delicacies upon their guests.

The first of the people from Lakuvi had arrived at a run, the messengers who had been sent for them barely managing to stay ahead of their eager guests.

They had news that cheered the whole village and put an end to Casca's worries. He had a horrifying mental picture of Savage's schooner sailing into the lagoon to rake the village with cannon fire, an aspect of warfare that had little attraction for him. In all his experience he had never found a practical defense against a cannonade. Neither running nor hiding was effective.

But the news from Lakuvi eased his mind. The messengers had arrived at the village shortly after Cakabau and his few survivors. The story of the battle for Navola had lost nothing in the telling.

In Cakabau's version the entire Navola village had been armed with muskets, scores of them. And muskets very much superior to those supplied by Savage, in that they could be reloaded in the blink of an eye. And Casca's three almost harmless mortar bursts had been described by Cakabau as coming from more and bigger guns than there were in the British fort at Levuka.

On hearing the news, Savage had cut free his anchors and raced away from the island with all possible sail set.

Casca smiled hugely as he clapped his hands to receive the *bilo* of kava.

The feasting went on all night, one earth oven after another being opened until everyone of the defeated enemy had been cooked.

By the time the sun came up every last morsel of the cooked meat had been eaten and the inevitable orgy was in full swing. By the time the sun went down again every man had enjoyed five or six or more women, and every woman at least a like number of men.

The orgy took some days to get over.

The *bilo* passed endlessly, the seductions proceeded apace, although with less and less frenzy, and perhaps even more enjoyment.

Casca reflected on his buried bottle of whiskey, wondered if Semele and perhaps some others had one hidden, too, and prayed by all the gods that grew that they would keep them hid.

The two tribes of hereditary enemies were locked and intertwined in an embrace that would last for hundreds of years—as it already had for hundreds of hundreds of years.

But the only fights that Casca saw were amongst the children, who brawled like drunken sailors, formed little armies, laid seige, set ambushes, and generally so enjoyed themselves that Casca was frankly envious.

But the ladies of Lakuvi were a great consolation for the loss of the joys of boyhood battlegrounds.

CHAPTER TWENTY-TWO

After several days some semblance of normalcy began to return to the everyday lives of the two peoples.

Husbands and wives gravitated toward each other. Casca found himself walking Vivita home past the little clusters of young women who put themselves in his way. In couples and in family groups the people of Lakuvi drifted back to their own village, and after another few days it was as if the great battle and the enormous feast had never happened.

Except for the songs. The entire history of the attack—the tactics of the defense, the sabotage of the canoes, the massacre and the feast that followed, the friendship with the village of Lakuvi—was recorded in a series of songs which would be sung in the village for many decades, maybe for centuries, and certainly for as long as their lessons remained valuable.

In all of these songs Casca was the mighty hero, the powerful Valangi who had come to the island at the behest of the gods to preserve the village and its people, to vanquish its enemies.

Casca accepted without demur his role as an emissary of the gods, but had been careful to ensure that he was taken for mortal and not himself held to be a god. He'd taken his share of blows and cuts in the fighting, and had been seen to bleed, although he'd been careful to conceal the speed at which his wounds healed.

His status in the councils of the village had risen. He now found himself almost always in a position of honor, along with Semele and Mbolo. He seemed to be brought into most of the discussions of village problems, his opinion sought in matters of building, farming, fishing, and other topics in which he had no real knowledge or interest.

But to decline giving an opinion would be rude, to offer a trite one would be absurd, so day after day he found that he was in fact applying more and more of his energies and intellect to management of the village.

If the realities of a farming problem eluded him, he would join the farmers the next day and help to implement whatever solution had been agreed upon, learning in the process just why the particular approach had been accepted and reappraising its effectiveness in light of what he learned.

In building matters, especially the vital fortifications and water storage, he was already adept, and he effected numerous significant improvements in these areas, and even small ones in the building of huts and the construction and drainage of steps and pathways. In addition he became an expert fisherman and a good diver, although he could not develop the phenomenal capacity to stay underwater which seemed almost natural to many of the villagers.

One night he looked up from an intense discussion to catch an amused half smile on Vivita's face. He looked at her questioningly and her glance flitted to Semele and Mbolo and their wives, the ultimate authority in the village.

Casca saw that they were sitting back in a sort of contented withdrawal, and he suddenly realized he was running the show. Imperceptibly Semele had led him to this point where he was in fact functioning as deputy chief of the tribe.

"Hold on there, boy," he mumbled to himself, "this job is not for you. You could be stuck here forever."

At the same instant the thought struck him that the island was not such a bad place to be stuck, and that unless something extraordinary happened he well could be stuck on it for a damn long time.

"Gotta get myself organized to get the fuck out of here," he mumbled again.

For the rest of the evening he strove to ensure that he didn't get drawn further into Semele's role.

Certainly it was time for him to be moving on. Most certainly he did not wish to become supreme chief of the village and spend the rest of his life as Semele did, mediating disputes between neighbors, guiding village discussions of farming, fishing, building, and the most mundane matters, playing host to visitors, being the butt of the children's unending pranks—and incidentally, preserving the village economy and seeing to its defense.

The scope of the job and the detailed, tedious, endless involvement appalled Casca. And the rewards—occasional deference, once in a while a special feast of turtle meat, the tastiest parts of defeated enemies, first access to most of the village virgins—fell a long way short of making the job attractive.

Nor was there any way that even the most astute operator could increase these rewards. Even Cakabau received little more. Money was almost unknown, and there was no way to spend it outside the city of Levuka.

If, say, Cakabau were to leave the islands, taking with him all the available cash, he might manage to spend a few riotous weeks in London, then return to find he'd been forgotten, his empire broken up, his palace occupied or in ruins. The power and prestige of a chief in these islands depended entirely upon the continuous use of that power for the benefit of his people. A chief could enrich all his people, and so himself, but it was not possible for himself to get rich at their expense.

It was this lack of sensibly civilized reward that convinced Casca that for all their sophistication in some things, the islanders were but simple savages, and that he should look elsewhere to spend more time of his seemingly endless life.

He could see now that there was real danger he might be made chief. No matter what the topic under discussion, Semele always made a place for him closest to himself.

The present topic was the erection of a new temple, a matter of total unconcern to Casca, yet as happened more and more frequently, he found himself at the center of this discussion too.

The old temple had been destroyed in the same hurricane that had brought the *Rangaroa* to the island, and until now more pressing matters had prevented the application of the necessary time and thought to its reconstruction.

Casca went to study the ruins of the temple, and stared at the idols lying scattered about. Most of these belonged outside the holy structure and were in their more or less normal position, except that several of them had been knocked over by the collapse of the temple framework.

The great central pole still stood rigidly vertical, its elaborate carvings rising about forty feet above the ground. Around it there had once been a thatched roof and walls that completely concealed the carvings and some stone gods now exposed to view. The hurricane had torn away the temple walls, the thatch roof, and the great, long poles that formed the forty-foot-high roof frame.

Around the outside of the temple there were numerous other carved idols of stone, of the wood used for war clubs, and of the soft tree ferns found in the depths of the jungle.

The ruined temple received scant attention from the villagers, and the gods little respect. Since the idols lay conveniently on their sides they were used like park benches. Friends who happened to meet near them would sit on them and chat, and the village children played on them. Had there been dogs, Casca didn't doubt they would have pissed on them.

Casca gathered that once completed, the new temple would be similarly ignored. The village gods, it seemed, were simply there, and that was that. They played no part, and were not invited into the ordinary affairs of the village.

Nor did the villagers presume to concern themselves with the affairs of their gods.

Casca sat down on a great carved head. No, he thought, this doesn't look like the place for the Messiah to make his next call.

The temple became the main topic of the meetings in the chief's house. From here and there around the room came scraps of information, practical and impractical suggestions, jokes, banter, and idle, irrelevant gossip.

One man said that his share of the roof thatch would be cut and delivered into the village before the moon was full. But various others—there seemed to be many—said they could not deliver the thatch until the moon had waned, some said to half. Various other men gave varying times for delivery of the poles for the framework for the walls and roof.

Semele listened with equal respect and attention to every speaker, and asked his usual slow, casual, but pointed questions.

Lanata, the new farmer chief, was sitting next to Semele, and he gave a little speech that brought laughter from all around the room.

It seemed the farmers who would be late with their share of the thatch were those who, during the planting season, had preferred to spend their time fishing, as a school of large grouper had appeared just outside the reef. Lanata wagged his finger at these farmers, holding them up to ridicule before the rest of the village as a bad example and a warning of how neglect of duty by a few could inconvenience or harm the whole village.

The offenders laughed as readily as any as their dereliction was paraded, but Casca got the impression that it might be some years before they again let the early part of a planting season slip by.

Dukuni, the fisherman chief, suggested that if they really enjoyed fishing so much, they should join the fishermen when there were no fat, lazy, easy-to-catch grouper. Every tiny fish had to be worked for, and any sort of catch came only after long hours of tedious waiting and repeated disappointments.

The demolition of the old temple now became a matter of paramount importance, for reasons Casca didn't know. A huge hole was now excavated all around the central pole, and as the hole deepened, all the huskiest men—including Semele and Mbolo—would jump down into it and try to free the pole from the remaining earth.

Casca joined in the competition. At first the efforts were playful, merely ceremonial, the dislodging of the great buried length being nearly impossible. But as the diggers exposed each new carved head, the efforts became more serious, and eventually Casca discerned that they were getting to the point where it might be possible for a man to heft free the post's length of something like sixty feet.

There was a frightful stench in the bottom of the hole, which grew stronger as more and more of the pole was exposed. Casca's inquiry about it was met with a blank stare and the simple reply: *"Te kanaka*—the man."

So, a dead man was buried with the pole. Well, that didn't surprise Casca too much. But he wondered if the building of the new temple would wait upon the death of somebody in the village. Presumably it would be an honor to be so buried, and such an honor might be reserved for someone of importance. Mbolo, for example, was certainly honored, but he was clearly in the best of health and spirits as Casca watched him heaving mightily at the pole from the bottom of the hole.

Casca was pretty sure that he himself was the strongest man in the village, as he normally was wherever he went. It also seemed to him that luck would play a considerable part, since once there was little enough of the pole still buried to make its removal possible, each successive try would be of assistance to the next in freeing up the earth's hold on the pole.

He wanted to win, as he would have wished to win any such test of strength, but he had a deeper reason. In his determination to avoid the job of chief, Casca had now adopted a pushy, ambitious sort of demeanor, seeking preferment and self-promotion wherever it was offered, making it evident, he thought, that he was of that unreliable type, the kind easily corrupted by a small taste of power. He hoped to win this contest of strength and then strut and swagger about the village so insufferably that the villagers would not only not consider him for Semele's job, but would be pleased to assist him when he announced his intention to depart the island.

Luck was on his side. The great carved pole was now teetering slightly in the imprisoning earth, each successive tryer easing it slightly more as he strove to wrench it free.

Casca liked the imagery of the shouts of encouragement for each contestant. As he climbed down into the sinking hole people shouted to him: "Take it away from him, Casca. Make him let it go, Casca." And as he felt it move at its base, everybody roared: "Let it go, dead man, Casca is stronger than you."

To Casca, in the bottom of the fetid hole, it almost did seem that he was wrestling with the dead man for possession of the pole, and with a mighty effort of arms and shoulders and back and legs he lifted it free of the earth and held it erect for a moment, to let it fall against the slope of the other side of the hole.

There was an enormous round of cheering, and Casca saw Mbolo where the pole rested against the side of the hole, beckoning him to climb up the carvings.

Casca was only too pleased to do so. The now open grave emitted a stench as foul as any he had ever known, and he was pleased to escape it.

Mbolo greeted him at the top of the hole and placed his arms around the pole as high as he could reach, seizing it himself a little lower while Semele grabbed it behind him. All the other contestants were leaping into the pit. When everybody had a firm hold, the drums and a chant started up, everybody heaved, and with a great rush the length of the pole came up. Many more hands grabbed for it above the ground, and in a few minutes all sixty feet of it was lying alongside the hole. This part of the job done, the actual building of the temple would not occur until the farmers could deliver the promised materials.

Casca, followed by all the others, ran for the cleansing ocean and threw himself into the shallows, scouring his flesh with handfuls of the dense, black sand, washing away the horrible odor of old death.

When they came out of the water there were women waiting with vessels of fragrant oils. Once annointed and sweet smelling, Casca began immediately upon his new campaign of strut and swagger. But when he saw Vivita's glance of contempt and disgust, he modified the act a little. It was not part of his plan to make himself a figure for ridicule.

CHAPTER TWENTY-THREE

That night Setole sat opposite him, grinning pleasantly, and Casca reflected how much he enjoyed the company of this placid, jolly woman. She was a fountain of good sense, and even among people as fun loving as the islanders, her happy enthusiasm for life was outstanding.

Now that he had some real command of the language, Casca found he enjoyed her company more and more. She had a fund of witty anecdotes about everyday life in the village, and was an unfailing source of wry and amusing stories.

But Casca was taken severely aback when he realized that Vivita had perceptibly withdrawn from their usual intimacy, that none of the younger women seemed to be trying for him tonight, and it looked as if Setole intended to take him home with her.

More than ever Casca felt like a pawn in this game amongst the women, and he cast about for some way to avoid being carted away by the fat woman like some fairground prize.

"Dammit," he said to himself, "I'm a fucking big wheel in this town, a hero, the war chief, damn near supreme chief. How come I get stuck with this fat old broad?"

But short of holding Setole off with his .38, Casca knew there was no way out. He considered rudely insulting her by brutally declining to accompany her, but he liked her too much to do that. She was honoring him. She had asserted herself to win him from Vivita, he had unwittingly gone along with that part of the game, and now he was stuck with the result. There was nothing for it but to put on the best face possible, suffer through the night, and be more careful in future.

Quite apart from these noble sentiments, Casca was also pretty sure that if he reneged on the deal, the game among the women might take a different turn, and he could find himself without a woman at all.

Setole proved to be as pleasant in bed as she was in conversation. Her enormous body was mainly muscle, and her agility and flexibility were really extraordinary. She was able to open her great legs as wide as any skinny little girl, and her superb musculature enabled her to use her sexual equipment as tightly, ingeniously, and excitingly as any of the thousands of women Casca had known.

Which was fine in the dark, but in the morning he awakened to a distinct shock to find himself lying like a pigmy alongside the huge upholstery of her body.

It was a further shock to discover that he had moved in.

Setole prepared his breakfast and gave him a fresh *sulu*, taking his other one to launder. She brushed his jacket, oiled his sandals, and most ominous of all, set aside almost half the hut for his exclusive use, laying fresh grass mats and spreading upon them Casca's personal possessions— his duffel, shaving gear, toothbrush, and comb, all of which had somehow materialized from the hut he had shared with Vivita.

"Great Hector's asshole," Casca cursed, "I don't want a fucking wife. And if I must have one, I'd rather have Vivita."

With the passing of each night the problem worsened. Neither Vivita nor any other woman now made any attempt to pry Casca loose from Setole. They were regarded like a married couple.

Casca still enjoyed the giant woman's company, and indeed enjoyed her in bed enormously. But he chafed at the situation and began to plan seriously toward his departure from the island.

He might wait for years before another ship called at the island, and then it might be a heavily armed slaver that would be difficult to capture and even more difficult for him to sail, with his more than likely reluctant crew.

Certainly none of the islanders knew anything of schooner sailing, and he felt sure that now that he was "married," they would vigorously oppose his departure. Clearly he would have to make his own way from the island which meant stealing one of the village boats.

So Casca began to bend his energies to learning everything he could about handling the sail canoes.

His sudden passion for fishing caused neither comment nor suspicion, even though he made a point of going out in all the worst weather to be encountered.

His status as war chief had been further exalted by his role as Semele's virtual deputy, and further again by his marital connection with Setole, a powerful woman herself in the village hierachy, and Mbolo's sister.

Even without these advantages he might not have been troubled much. Every villager virtually organized his own life, farming or fishing, building or diving, more or less as his own circumstances and whim dictated.

Casca became an expert sail handler, then a proficient helmsman, and then he set himself to learn all he could of navigation.

He especially liked to join those fishermen who worked in the depths of the night, and he questioned them endlessly about the way through the stars.

In time he came to know that he would be on course for the distant island of Lifou if he kept Orion—to Casca a Roman legionnaire, to the islanders a beautiful woman dancing—behind him. He should also steer between the Giant Shrimp, which he knew as Scorpio, and the Albatross, which sailors called the Southern Cross.

Casca decided upon the boat that he needed—a small sail canoe with a single outrigger, one triangular sail, and a small covered area protected by thatch and tapa cloth. He was confident that he could sail this vessel single-handed, and he seized upon every possible chance to practice with it.

As the fishermen became accustomed to Casca's presence among them they gradually lost interest in which boat he sailed in, where he went, and what he caught. Some days he would linger on the beach until all the fishermen had left, and then set out by himself in whatever craft happened to be available. There were plenty of boats, and different ones were used on different days, according to the weather and the type fish being sought.

The small sail canoes were mainly used in the hunt for big-game fish way offshore, and when these fish were not plentiful Casca was often able to spend the day sailing alone.

A huge school of grouper arrived off the reef, and almost all of the fishermen preferred to hang by the reef in the paddle canoes angling for the large fish that bit readily on any sizable bait. A number of other fishermen worked inside the lagoon, seeking bait fish.

Several sail canoes were unused, and Casca took the smallest and sailed it to the western end of the island, where he ran it into the quiet backwater below the place of refuge.

He climbed the cliff and returned to the village, arriving about sunset.

In the chief's house that night Dukuni and a few other fishermen greeted him, boasting of their catches of giant grouper.

"Maybe I should have gone in your boat today," Casca responded. But he did not volunteer, and was not asked, just how he had spent the day.

Several days passed before the boat was missed, and then, as with all such events, the theft was blamed on a sneak thief from the enemy village of Lakuvi.

When he was not out sailing in the small craft Casca spent a great deal of time carrying coconuts, breadfruit, and sweet potatoes to the place of refuge.

He became very adept at racing along the narrow cliff

path, juggling a heavy tapa sack on one shoulder as he looked down hundreds of feet to the rocks and waves below, or up the sheer face of the cliff to the peak above the refuge.

To get to the cliff edge above the backwater he had to pass Tepole's body, now a stinking, pulpy mass that would yet take some time for the benign jungle to consume. There were on the island no jackals or dogs or cats, and the only rats stayed by the villages, where they had come ashore from Clevinger's ships. It fell to the insects to clean up what was left of the mess that Tepole had made of his life.

Farther away he could see where Sonolo still sat in his self-imposed exile, waiting for death. Or was he already dead? Casca couldn't tell from this distance, and chose to ignore the stonelike man.

He enjoyed stepping down the near precipitous cliff face to where he stashed his supplies on the lee shore of the little backwater sheltered by the expanse of flat rock which rose several feet above the sea. The rock was always dry, and it seemed that only a freak wave ever broke across it to enter the little backwater.

In a week he accumulated a huge cache of food and coconuts, including a crock full of pickled grouper flesh and several more crocks of fresh water. He also cached a musket, a powder horn, shot, and his bottle of whiskey.

The moon was waxing fast, and Casca planned to sail on the night that it filled. He hoped to be off to the island of Lifou four or five days later.

He was, by dint of great experience, a capable navigator. He had already been practicing the craft, albeit mainly on land, for a thousand six hundred years, when the British Navy turned the craft into a science with Greenwich Mean Time, standard nautical tables, meticulously accurate chronometers, the sextant, and eventually the detailed Admiralty charts that showed almost every headland, cape, island, islet, reef, and known depth on the surface of the planet.

But now he was introduced to the practice of navigation as an art.

The islanders used only one instrument—song. There was a song for every possible destination, including even the land where the yellow people live, although none of the islanders had ever sailed to China and only a few Chinese traders had ever visited the island.

Every islander knew every one of the songs, and at the appropriate times of the day, according to the season and the winds and the weather, they sang the appropriate verses of the song that recorded the way that led through the stars, the changes of wave patterns caused by islands and reefs, the sorts of landscapes to be looked for, the known dangers, and every other piece of information a seafarer could put to use.

And now Casca knew the song that would take him to the island of Lifou. He had learned the hard way—by doing—but he learned well.

CHAPTER TWENTY-FOUR

The day finally arrived when the farmers of Navola had delivered the necessary materials to erect the temple.

Justly proud of the enormous strength that had won him the roles of pole lifter, Casca climbed into the new hole, the carvings on the pole providing footholds as he made his way down the length.

Standing on the bottom, he grasped the pole and hugged it to him, struggling to get it vertical. The task proved more difficult than he had expected. In the narrow confine of the bottom of the hole he could exert little purchase, and it took him some time to get it into the upright position.

As he did so there was a resounding cheer from above ground, and a slow chant commenced.

At the fourth beat Casca recognized the same chant that had launched the canoe, and an inkling of unease entered his mind.

At the fifth beat there was a mighty roar, within which Casca heard his own protesting voice, and a great cascade of sand poured into the hole from every side.

"Great Jupiter's balls," Casca shouted, "what the fuck's going on here?"

The rapid rain of sand continued falling and Casca could feel that it had already reached his knees. He strove frantically to move his legs, but could not even wriggle his toes.

Now the sand was rising a little more slowly as the taper of the hole widened, but inch by inch it moved up over his thighs. Buried to the crotch, wedged between the pole and the side of the hole, he could move nothing but his arms.

He reached as high as he could, found two handholds in the carvings, and tried to drag himself free of the imprisoning sand—a useless effort that accomplished nothing but his exhaustion.

He had been tricked.

Or had he?

He recalled the blunt answer when he had inquired about the stench at the bottom of the hole of the old temple. He had assumed some spiritual reason for the burial of a doubtless revered man with the pole of the temple. It had not occurred to him, as it did now, that a live man provided a very practical means of keeping the pole vertical while the hole was filled around it. And yes, he was doubtless considered worthy of the honor.

The sand was now up around his chest, and he was pouring forth every curse and oath and imprecation he could lay his tongue to.

Then his breath began to falter, his chest constricted by the pressure of the sand.

For one of the very few times in his long life Casca wanted to beg. But he quickly realized that it was pointless. Nothing he could say could possibly be heard through the chanting and drumming above ground. So he went back to cursing.

The sand continued to fall. Now only his head was free, uptilted along the pole toward the daylight.

The chanting stopped.

A single frangipani blossom came floating down to settle on his face, and he heard Vivita's voice: *"Vanaka, vanaka*—thank you, thank you."

Then a roaring chorus from the entire village: *"Vanaka! Vanaka!"* He gulped a great breath of flower-scented air, and a great rush of sand buried his head.

He would die once more—but for how long this time?

CHAPTER TWENTY-FIVE

The whole island trembled. The mountain steamed, sprayed out ash and sand, and finally spewed forth a great river of boiling mud and rock.

The stream of molten lava coursed down the mountainside to the sea, where it plunged in amidst tremendous clouds of steam.

By night the river glowed red and the mountain shot brilliant glowing colors into the sky.

The ocean raged and the waters of the lagoon heaved up and inundated the land, big waves rushing up the hillsides and swamping the village. Then it retreated back to the lagoon and beyond, back over the reef and into the ocean. It scoured out the village as it left, sucking along with it everything it encountered.

The wave retreated outside the reef, leaving most of the lagoon dry behind it. Huge fish, giant squid, and enormous rays such as the villagers had never dreamed existed, lay panting on the dry bottom.

Then another giant wave came booming over the reef, refilling the lagoon as it raced to the shore, where its towering height crashed down upon the village like a great hammer, flattening everything before it and then retiring again, sucking whole houses, people, canoes, even the sturdy palisades into the lagoon and beyond, over the reef and out into the ocean.

Over and over the cycle was repeated. Great sharks and groupers, never seen inside the reef, were dumped inside the remains of the village. For two days and nights the volcano spurted fire and lava; the island heaved and the ocean raged.

Then on the third morning all was quiet.

The village was devastated. Not a house was standing and all three palisades had disappeared, as had the great chief's house. Where the new temple had stood surrounded by its gods, there was now nothing but a great hole. The huge roof pole had disappeared along with most of the stone idols.

Semele had disappeared along with about a hundred others. Mbolo moved about the ruins of the village, tending to the survivors, doing what he could for the many broken arms and legs and heads.

Suddenly the ruined village was filled with the excited shrieks of the children. Unconcerned with the death and destruction all around them, the little ones were gamboling about on the beach, marveling upon the wonders that had been washed up from the depths, when they came upon Casca.

Their yells brought the whole village running, to cluster about the dead man whose arms still obstinately clutched the carvings of the post, as he had in his last desperate attempt to heave himself free. Locked to the pole like this, the corpse had ridden the pole back and forth a dozen times from the village to the ocean and back to the beach.

Mbolo moved to gently pry loose the clutching fingers, and started back in alarm.

The rest of the villagers retreated several paces and waited.

Mbolo gingerly approached again and touched Casca's arm. It was unmistakable—the corpse was cold, but nowhere near as cold as it should have been. Fresh blood showed around the body's many bruises and cuts. Mbolo laid his head to Casca's back and listened. There was no sign of breathing, but Mbolo thought he detected life. He turned and shouted.

"Fire, fire, make fire here. Quickly, quickly. Big fire here. Another one here." He pointed to places on the ground to either side of Casca's body as he squatted beside him and commenced a powerful massage.

In the hole Casca's breathing had shut down as he exhaled his last lungful of air through his nose in his last conscious act. His next attempt to breath blocked his nose and mouth with earth, and suffocation quickly followed.

Or rather, something between hibernation and suspended animation, as the curse of the dying Jesus took effect and the process of cell decay was arrested, the heart and lungs and other organs lowering their activity to virtually zero.

The first gigantic heave of the earth had thrust the pole up out of the ground, and the first of the tsunami waves had floated the pole and Casca out to sea. The many trips back and forth had sluiced out his nose and mouth with seawater, clearing the air passages.

Now Mbolo's vigorous massage and the heat of the fires reactivated his body's systems, and he drew a short, shuddering breath.

The watching villagers ran away in terror as Mbolo continued the massage, but crept cautiously back as Casca drew another, longer breath. The huge islander continued the treatment until Casca was breathing deeply and regularly. Then he moistened Casca's lips with water, covered him with tapa cloths, squatted beside him and waited.

CHAPTER TWENTY-SIX

The earthquake knocked over the squatting Sonolo, awakening him from his deep trance.

He picked himself up and looked around in wonder. The whole world was rocking back and forth, trees were crashing to the ground, there was deafening noise, and ashes and glowing cinders of rock were falling from the sky.

Sonolo watched in wonder. His wonder increased when he glanced down and saw his own body. His skin hung in empty folds, the huge muscles and the layer of fat having wasted away. Through the slack envelope of skin Sonolo could see his bones. He looked like a dead man.

How had this happened? Why was he here on the rock of refuge? Had he been exiled from the village? For what crime? What had he done?

Slowly, in tattered fragments, pieces of his experience came back to him.

He suddenly recalled the modern English city Levuka, with its paved roads, and great, four-legged beasts that men rode on, and other four-legs that ran at these beasts' heels making a fearful noise.

Then he remembered the only four-legged animals he knew, the rats casually imported in the holds of Clevinger's ship, and he recalled the days when he was a little boy and Clevinger had been trading from the island.

He had fond memories of the defrocked New England parson who had not only taught him to speak English, but also to read and write, and who had especially impressed upon him the evils of whiskey.

With an awful, wrenching shock Sonolo recollected his drunken murder of his life-long friend, comrade, and rival, his cousin Sakuvi. He looked down at his wasted body and assumed that he, too, was dead, and was glad of it.

A sweet memory came to him of his wife and his three children, and then of his old mother, and of his dead father.

He looked around. Clevinger, preacher turned rationalist, was right. There was no life after death, or else his father would be here to greet him.

He wondered how long he'd been dead, how old his children might now be, and whom his wife might have married?

He had no qualms about the welfare of his family. He did not even have a concept of need, nor of loneliness.

The awful thought struck him that, as there was no life after death, he was stuck here forever by himself. Forever, whatever that was. But if there were no life after death, what state was he in?

"Dammit it," he shouted in English, the way Clevinger used to when he was annoyed. "I never could understand anything of that after death business when I was alive. And now I'm dead, and I still don't understand it. Damn and blast."

The memory of the forest of masts of the scores of ships in Levuka harbor brought him back to the arrival at Navola of the Reverend Clevinger's ship.

The mad, defrocked parson had been a godsend for the village, for all the villages he visited. He robbed them of everything they possessed of any value, but it cost them nothing, for that was the value they put on all of it.

They had been lucky. Throughout the South Pacific the names of the merchant-adventurer missionaries had become bywords for avarice, lechery, cruelty, ruthlessness, and hypocrisy: Burns, Philip, Clevinger, Savage, Boyd,

Hedstrom, Bentley. They combined missionary zeal with slaving, trading, and exploitation on a gigantic scale.

Clevinger cheated the natives like the rest, but he carried no Bible and no musket, and did not deal in slaves. He traded worthless baubles for priceless treasures, but unlike the others, he did not claim that he had been sent by God. Where his competitors handed out Bibles, the ex-parson handed out temperance and rationalist tracts, and taught English so that the natives might better appreciate the dire warnings of the evils of strong drink.

When he sailed away he left behind rats, fleas, mosquitoes, a quite unwarranted belief in the efficacy of steel rather than stone tools, an intense interest in mirrors and bangles and beads, and an urgent craving to sample the proscribed horrors of the whiskey bottle.

Sonolo remembered his warning: "Man need not die to enter heaven or hell, he can find them here. And hell is always waiting in the bottom of the bottle."

Sonolo looked glumly around the refuge. "I have found the hell I went looking for, and now what am I to do?"

CHAPTER TWENTY-SEVEN

Consciousness returned slowly. Casca awoke from terrifying dreams of entombment to see the fuzzy outline of Mbolo's face floating above him. He gasped and sank back into unconsciousness as Mbolo again moistened his lips.

When he woke again Mbolo's face was clear in his vision, but he could remember nothing. He sank back to sleep once more, this time into a quiet slumber.

He woke again from nightmare, and in a frenzy tried to rise. Mbolo restrained him gently and calmed him, holding him like a child in his great arms and putting a bowl of thin fish soup to his lips.

Casca sipped, then sucked greedily at the liquid, gulping it down. In a moment he vomited it all up and sank back to sleep again.

When next he woke he was lying on a grass mat in what remained of Setole's house, Mbolo's face still above him. He eagerly drank another bowl of soup and motioned for more.

Setole, Vivita, and Mbolo nursed him for several days, and at last he was able to sit up, then to stand. Finally, leaning on Setole's and Vivita's arms, he could walk.

"Now," said Mbolo, "we know who you are. You are the great, white bearded one whose coming has been foretold for countless generations. You are Rangaroa, the man-god."

"I sure as hell am not, Mbolo. You've seen me bleed. I'm no god. I don't even have a beard, and when I do, it ain't white."

Mbolo smiled in quiet triumph. "Yes, I have seen that your wounds do bleed, but I have also seen that they heal very quickly, and I have wondered about that. You came to us in the hurricane that destroyed our old temple. Your ship bore your name, Rangaroa, the god of the sea. You were buried alive in the new temple and survived, and you survived the earthquake and the great wave. And not one of the many women you have lain with is with child, while many of our women are pregnant to the men who came with you. And you do have a beard. And it is white."

Casca's hand shot to his face. There was a stubble of beard. Damn, of course his beard had continued to grow in the grave. But white?

Yes. He knew of this too. More than once he had dug out men who had been buried alive, and their hair and their beard had turned stark white. He didn't need a mirror to know that this had happened to him too.

"We are very pleased to have you return to us as god and chief, now that Semele had gone."

"Dammit, Mbolo!" Casca shouted desperately. "You're the biggest and the oldest and the most experienced man in the village—you should be the chief."

Mbolo smiled tolerantly. "This is not possible, for I am above the chief."

For a moment Casca tried to see the point of what he thought was a joke. Then he realized that Mbolo was not joking. While it was Semele who conducted all discussions, weighed information, and pronounced decisions, nothing was ever decided contrary to Mbolo's view.

"Above the chief? What's your job anyway?"

Mbolo's patient smile lit up his placid face. "Clevinger used to say that Semele was the king and me the pope."

"High priest!" Casca exclaimed in confusion. "But I never see you about any priestly duties."

"Duties?"

"Yeah, like preaching at people, or praying to the gods, stuff like that."

Again Mbolo smiled, and he spoke to Casca as he might have spoken to an intelligent but unobservant child.

"My only duty is to see that we do not try to move the world in ways contrary to the way of the great spirit that moves all."

"And this great spirit tells you that I should be chief?"

"No. It is clear that you must be chief."

Casca groaned. Why the hell hadn't he made his escape when he had it all organized?

The contest of strength with the temple pole. His mania to show that he was the strongest man in the village had put him in this position. Again.

Don't you ever learn, Casca? he asked himself. He shrugged. "Nothing to do but go with it," he muttered to himself. Aloud he said: "So I'm to be king and you the pope."

"No," said Mbolo. "That is what Clevinger said, it is not how it is. We are a family, and you are like the man of the family, and I like the woman."

"With the woman above the man?"

"Of course, yes."

"Hmm. Maybe I am beginning to see. How much time was I in the ground?" he asked.

"In the ground and in the sea twice a night and a day, and we found you today," Mbolo answered.

Casca smiled. Then he saw Mbolo smiling back, and quickly mastered his features. But inwardly he was grinning happily. The sail canoe and his stash of provisions might yet be in place. He could escape tonight or tomorrow. Very well. For now he would go along with the game, playing the cards he had been dealt.

He nodded to Mbolo. To himself he thought, So, I'm god. Well, it's not the first time!

CHAPTER TWENTY-EIGHT

Casca's coronation ceremony took up the greater part of a day and a night.

Everybody, including a number of guests from Lakuvi, gathered at the chief's newly built house shortly after dawn. Mbolo sat in the place of highest honor, Casca next to him, the *tabua* on its long cord leading from Mbolo's feet to the huge bowl of kava.

Mbolo accepted the first bowl of kava, draining it, clapping and pronouncing it empty. The young warrior accepted the *bilo* and returned to the bowl to refill it. Mbolo rose and moved aside, motioning for Casca to occupy the position by the whale's tooth.

Casca sat and looked along the cord to the kava bowl, then around the great room at the entire population of the village. The *bilo* arrived and he clapped, accepted, and drank it.

Every voice in the house said *"matha"* with him, and every pair of hands clapped three times with him. Again he looked along the cord to the kava bowl and then around the room.

"I feel like a king on his throne," he muttered to himself in some amazement. His glance roved back around the room and came to rest on Mbolo, squatting beside him.

"No, I don't. Dammit, I feel like the father of a family."

A great wellspring of affection for his people filled his being, along with an all-pervasive contentment.

"Maybe I'll just keep the job for a while and see what sort of a fist I can make of it. I don't have to move on just yet." He settled down to enjoy the occasion.

The *bilo* of kava passed back and forth to each of the minor chiefs, then their wives, then, to the whole of the rest of the tribe in some order that Casca could no way discern. Mbolo made a long, long speech, followed by Ateca. Then each of the minor chiefs made long speeches, too, followed by their wives, and then from all around the room speaker followed speaker, apparently at random, until virtually every villager, certainly somebody from every family, had spoken on the accession of the new chief.

Meanwhile, banana-leaf platters of fish and taro and cassava and breadfruit passed around and around the great house. Just when Casca was convinced that he could not eat another mouthful, the supply of food would diminish and the *bilo* of kava would be passed again, the speeches continuing.

After two or three hours of drinking kava more food appeared, now some huge crabs, papayas, mangoes, and bananas, then lobsters, eventually a giant turtle. Each successive course of the banquet followed a long interval of kava drinking and speech making.

Casca enjoyed the occasion immensely. He was now very much bigger than the hard, lean railroad worker who had arrived on the island a few months earlier, and his appetite had increased accordingly. Without effort he put away everything that was placed before him. He had also become attuned to the effects of the kava, and after a few *bilos*, passed into an enjoyable state of alert tranquility which grew more and more pleasant with each *bilo* he drank.

Finally, very late in the night, the speeches came to an end and people drifted out of the house. The minor chiefs and their wives withdrew, and Casca found himself the only man in the room.

Setole was nearby, her enormous bulk seated on a mat

alongside Casca. Next to her sat Ateca, and there were also a score or more other women present, Vivita seemingly first among them.

Setole went to the raised, private part of the room and prepared a sleeping mat, indicating that she was doing so for Casca. He watched in some amusement and a little amazement as she then prepared a mat for herself on the small floor close to the dais.

On the other side of the room, and just as close, Vivita spread a mat. A little farther away Ateca laid out a mat, and then in some sort of unperceivable order, each of the other women did the same, keeping a respectful distance from each other so that they were distributed all around the room.

Casca looked around. Except for Semele's widow, each of these women had slept with him at some time since he'd been in the village. He realized with a start that each of the girls he'd slept with in the village of Lakuvi was there, too, even the ones he'd forgotten that he had slept with during the orgy following Cakabau's defeat.

"Great man-eating pussy of Venus," Casca groaned, "they surely don't expect me to service all of them tonight. I might be getting a bit too old for this sort of caper."

As it turned out, he slipped into a blissful, kava-stoned sleep as soon as he lay on his grass mat and slept through the night undisturbed.

In the days that followed, he found that the pattern of his life had been drastically altered. He was only safe so long as he stayed on his raised dais. As soon as he stepped down from it one or other of his wives—it seemed that all of them were now his—would assail him to sit with her, to allow her to prepare a meal for him and if it were night, to make love to her.

And his wives were the least of it. It seemed that everybody in the village had a problem of some sort and an urgent need to lay it at Casca's feet. It even seemed to him that several villagers invented or resurrected old problems for the simple pleasure of presenting them to him.

He discovered that wherever he went in the rebuilt village or in the recultivated farm patches or on the newly made fishing boats, there was work for him to do, advice to be given, problems to be solved, decisions to be made, quarrels and disputes to be arbitrated. And always there were children trying to trip him or frighten him or simply waylay him by forming a dancing chain around him. He would no sooner oblige them by stumbling over a stretched vine to their enormous delight, but would trip over a cunningly placed stick he hadn't seen, to their greatest glee. Whenever they jumped at him from concealment he would leap high into the air in simulated terror, and their shrieks of joy would scarcely cease when another of them might succeed in actually startling him, the merriment bursting out afresh.

Most nights either Setole or Vivita would usually lay claim to him, but every few nights they would yield to one of the other women. It irritated Casca immensely that even as supreme chief and god he still didn't get to choose his own bedmate.

His irritation increased further when he noticed that his wives, including Setole and Vivita, and even the elderly Ateca, left the chief's house to spend the night with other men whenever it suited them.

"Damn," he fumed, "I'm a hero, a war chief, supreme chief. I'm even God Almighty, but I don't get to choose who lays me, and my wives just lay anybody they please."

A few days and a few nights and Casca was once more thinking of flight.

He was sleeping with Vivita when it occurred to him that he preferred that she be the woman to whom he would bid good-bye, so he woke her gently and made love to her once more. When she fell back to sleep he snatched up his duffel, threw his few possessions into it, and crept from the house.

CHAPTER TWENTY-NINE

There was no moon, but Casca moved quickly and soon arrived at the place of refuge.

He was halfway across it, toward where Tepole's remains lay, when Sonolo rose up from the ground in front of him as Casca's footfalls woke him.

"*Mbula*, Casca," the ex-war chief greeted him. "Are you dead now too?"

Casca laughed aloud as he stared through the darkness at the emaciated man.

"No, Sonolo, I'm as alive as you are."

"But I am dead, Casca."

Casca reached out a hand and touched him on the chest. Sonolo started back as if burnt. His mouth dropped open in terror. Tentatively he stretched out one hand.

"Touch me," Casca invited. "I am real, just as you are." Sonolo's trembling hand touched his shoulder, withdrew, then touched him again.

"Then we are both alive?" Sonolo asked in wonder. "Then what has happened to me?"

Casca sat down and motioned to him to do the same. He took from the duffel some fruit and a coconut.

"You eat, and I'll try to explain," he said. He then quickly told him how the muskets had accomplished the defeat of Cakabau.

At this news Sonolo seemed to come to life. He hungrily munched the fruit thirstily from the coconut as Casca continued the story of the earthquake, Semele's death, his own return from the dead, and his chieftainship.

"Then I am not dead, nor in exile?" Sonolo asked wonderingly.

"Neither one," Casca answered. He saw opportunity and grasped it. "The village awaits you. I have come to tell you that you are to be chief."

"But you have just told me that you are chief, that you are Rangaroa come to lead us."

"Indeed," Casca replied, "but Rangaroa cannot stay for long in one village. There is much for me to do. The time has come for me to return to the sea, and you must take my place as chief."

"I do not understand."

Casca stood up. "Return to the village and consult with Mbolo. Tell him what I have said, and tell him the manner of my going, then you will understand. You will be a good chief. Good-bye. *Mbula.*"

He got up and strode quickly to the cliff. At the very edge he turned around. Sonolo had just gotten to his feet and was staring through the darkness toward him.

Casca waved his hand and dropped down the cliff face, crouching under the overhang of rock.

He heard Sonolo's startled shout, then he could hear him running toward the cliff to stop at the edge, shouting into the darkness: "Rangaroa, where are you? Casca, what has become of you?"

The confused Sonolo stood a little while at the cliff edge. There was just enough light for him to see that Casca's body had not crashed onto the rocks below, nor had he heard any fall. He looked around at the night sky. Had the man-god flown into the clouds where the Valangi came from? Perhaps Mbolo could explain.

He turned and headed back across the refuge and toward the village.

CHAPTER THIRTY

Casca heard Sonolo leave, and continued his climb down to the broad, flat rock. He made his way around the edge of the small backwater and found the sail canoe, riding the quiet water at the end of the vines that secured it to several trees.

He ran to where his provisions were hidden, and found, as he had hoped, that the tidal wave had not struck this side of the island. Everything was just as he'd left it.

He quickly loaded the supplies into the small boat, untied the lines, and pushed it out beyond the rock into the open sea.

From horizon to horizon all was one blackness, peppered with a few stars. Casca raised the sail and the offshore breeze carried him from the shore. Behind him he could just make out the mass of the cliff. Ahead there was an endless space, the few stars fading into the clouds that were gradually building toward a storm.

The wind died to a calm, and Casca sat just offshore in the tiny sail canoe. Now the last of the stars had disappeared and there was no light. He could no longer distinguish the shape of the cliff from the sea or the night sky.

It didn't matter. He just sat and waited, letting his destiny cast him adrift once more. . . .